CAPTURED BY THE BLACK SHADOW.

"Somebody is watching us through a spyglass!" Larry said.

"Exactly, and we don't want to disturb them."

"You're right, Josh. Tonight we'll just sack out by the fire here and tomorrow, after they see that we're friendly, we'll find the way up there."

They need not have worried about that. Whatever went around their faces, whatever unguent was in that cloth held to their noses, made everything dreamlike. When they awoke, their hands and feet were tightly bound, their heads were throbbing balls of pain, and, framed in the only light they could see, was the black shadow of some monstrous creature that babbled wild sounds. Both the boys moaned in total despair.

D1562552

THE SHIP THAT NEVER WAS

Mickey Spillane

BANTAM BOOKS
TORONTO · NEW YORK · LONDON · SYDNEY

RL 6, Il age 11 and up

THE SHIP THAT NEVER WAS
A Bantam Book / March 1982.

ISBN 0-553-20380-0

Published simultaneously in the United States and Canada

Bantam Books are published by Bantam Books, Inc. Its trade-
mark, consisting of the words "Bantam Books" and the portrayal
of a rooster, is Registered in U.S. Patent and Trademark Office
and in other countries. Marca Registrada. Bantam Books, Inc.,
666 Fifth Avenue, New York, New York 10103.

PRINTED IN THE UNITED STATES OF AMERICA

0 9 8 7 6 5 4 3 2

THE SHIP
THAT NEVER WAS

CHAPTER 1

The old man was a gaunt wreck, barely able to speak. The sun had leathered his skin and his mouth was a dry, parched thing, moving slowly, speaking without being able to be heard.

Larry and Josh pulled the old gray skiff all the way up on the sand and Josh said, "I'll get some water."

Larry nodded and looked back at the man they had just dragged out of the sea. "Take it easy, my friend. You'll be all right."

The man tried to smile, but his face was weathered tight and the skin tightened on his face. When Josh came back with the thermos of water from their boat, Larry let it dribble into the man's mouth slowly, then wet his face and hair.

Appreciatively, the man nodded and his voice croaked out a sound.

"What did he say?" Josh asked.

"I think he said thanks."

The occupant of the old skiff blinked, acknowledging. He took another sip of water, let the boys wet him down again, then smiled slowly and fell asleep.

As gently as they could, Larry Damar and Josh Toomey lifted the old man from the bottom of the wooden boat and wrapped him in the blankets from their own craft.

One hour ago they had been out on a leisurely cruise in the *Sea Eagle* with nothing on their minds when they spotted what they had thought to be a deserted boat floating low in the water.

Josh had said, "Hey, look at that over there."

"It's some kind of a boat."

"And it's sinking."

"Josh," Larry had said, "I think it's already sunk."

"Only halfway." Josh laughed. "Should we pull it in?"

"You want an old wreck?"

"That thing has pretty good lines on it. I bet your dad could tell us what it was modeled after."

"Maybe." Larry grinned. "Let's go look."

The skiff was old and it was sinking, but it had an occupant whose eyes looked at theirs and they had brought the boat to shore. Now they were fifty miles away from civilization with the survivor of an unknown wreck and they weren't quite sure what to do.

It took quite a while, but they made the old man as comfortable as they could, slinging him on a canvas hammock made from their motor cover, with a shade of palm fronds to keep the sun from him. When they were sure he was asleep, they went back to the skiff they had found him in and reread the name printed on it.

H.M.S. *TIGER*, it read, in faded black with a red-and-gold border. "This can't be real," Larry said.

"What does it mean?"

"The initials stand for *His Majesty's Ship,* but the British haven't made wooden boats like this for oceangoing ships in . . . well, a couple of hundred years."

"But it's only a skiff," Josh insisted.

Larry walked around it, studying its size and construction. It was an oaken lapstrake job, with cedar ribs and remnants of pine seats. In the bow, an open copper water cask had a green patina on its surface, and the forged iron fittings of the rudder were pitted and rusted with age.

"This isn't a skiff," Larry told his friend. "It's what they called a 'longboat,' a working utility boat they kept on the decks of galleons."

Josh seemed a little incredulous. "Larry . . . don't tell me this . . . this longboat has been floating around with that old man in it for a couple of hundred years."

"Not likely. You notice something funny?"

"What?"

"No wormholes. If this *had* been in the water any length of time, the teredo worms would have eaten it up."

"But it *had* to be left in the water. The seams leak, but not all that much." Josh paused and looked at his friend quizzically. "Unless it's been in fresh water."

"Here in the Caribbean?"

"Then what do you suggest?"

After a few moments' thought, Larry said, "They used to make movies down this way. Oh, the ships they used for British ships of the line and Spanish galleons were all converted from more modern hulls, but smaller boats like this would have been duplicated almost exactly."

Both of them fingered the aged wood, examining the cracks in the close grain and the warped ridges of the joints. Josh grinned slowly and said, "You don't really believe that, do you?"

Larry felt silly, but he shook his head. "No."

Then he let out a chuckle and added, "Maybe our passenger can give us some information."

But that didn't seem likely, not for many hours anyway. The boys managed to have him drink a little more water, but the old man went back to sleep immediately afterward. "I think we'll be camping out here tonight," Josh said.

Larry nodded. "I'll go radio Dad on Peolle Island and he can get the word over to your place."

"Should we call for help for the old man?"

"It would be dark by the time anybody got here," Larry replied. "Besides, he seems to be okay. Pretty worn out, but not in serious condition. Tomorrow we'll move him back to Peolle ourselves."

"What about his boat?" Josh asked.

"I have an idea that old boat is important somehow. Let's rig up a tow on it and get it back."

"You think it will stay in one piece?"

"Well, it has so far . . . and it looks like pretty sturdy equipment."

"Larry. . . ?"

"Yeah?"

"You remember those funny feelings I used to get when something strange was going to happen?"

Larry let out a grunt and said, "Look, how many times do I have to tell you that . . ."

But Josh cut him off. "My friend, you are a mainlander and I am an islander. We think different ways. In Miami, you were at home. Here, I am at home."

"Okay," Larry grinned, "I remember your funny feelings."

"Good, because I have them again."

Getting their survivor aboard the *Sea Eagle* wasn't as easy as the boys expected. Even as frail as he was, the old man was difficult to handle, but using their canvas and ropes, they managed to hoist him to the back deck and make him comfortable.

All this time he had kept his left arm pressed closely to his chest, and until they had him in the deck chair, they thought he had been injured. But in this new position, they realized what he was doing: Under the tattered rag of a shirt, he was pressing an old, dried-out leather purse against his ribs. When Larry went to move it, the old man's eyes filled with terror.

He made some guttural sounds, said some faint words in protest, and Larry smiled to show him no harm would be done and pulled a blanket around him.

"What did he say?" Josh asked.

"Beats me. It sounded like a foreign language."

"That last time he spoke ... when he said thanks ..."

"I said I *think* he said thanks. It wasn't what he said, but the way he said it. He sounded grateful."

"He sure thinks a lot of whatever's in that leather folder," Josh remarked.

"Probably all of his possessions."

"Yeah. Well, we better get going if we want to get home by evening. I put a snubber on the towline back there to ease the strain on the nylon. Now, if that boat just holds together ..."

"Only one way we'll find out," Larry said. He threw the clutch lever to forward, eased the throttle on, and pulled away from the beach. In their wake, Josh hauled the boat forward until it was riding the second wave. It held its position perfectly and Josh tied it in place.

Together, the boys watched it riding proudly back there, the water peeling back from its prow. They

were both thinking the same thing ... that longboat *could* be old and it *could* be hiding a great
secret, but they didn't build boats like that anymore.

Vincent Damar and Timothy Toomey made sure
the old man was in satisfactory condition and asleep
before they made coffee and looked out at their
sons, who were pulling the longboat up above the
high-water mark.

"What I can't understand," Vincent said, "is how
two kids like them can get involved in so many
unusual circumstances."

"They are curious, my friend. You, me ... well,
we might have figured that boat for a derelict and
never have bothered to look inside it."

"At least this time it was a simple rescue and not
something that sets the entire Caribbean on its
ear."

"You never can tell, Vincent."

"What's that supposed to mean?"

Timothy nodded toward their sleeping guest. "We
still don't know who he is. His language ... so
strange. Do you know it?"

A frown creased Vincent's brow and he chewed
his lip a moment. "There's something strange about
it ... and something mighty familiar too."

"Have you heard it before?"

"I don't know, Tim. It seems like I have, but I
can't tell where."

"Those papers ... the ones in the old leather
case ..."

"From the edges I saw, it's very old parchment.
They are handwritten documents done with a split
quill point, but unless I examine them carefully,
there's no way I can tell what language they're in."

"I wish I had your education, my friend."

"You have," Vincent told him, "but your education is in the ways of the island. Look at how much I've learned from you."

"We all learn from each other." He paused a second, then: "How do you plan to learn the old man's identity?"

"There is one way," Vincent said. "We'll wait until he's strong enough to talk, then make a tape recording of him and send it to the Language Institute in Miami. Somebody there will certainly identify it and after that, it's just a case of getting an interpreter here."

"We could sail him there."

"Let's wait until he's awake. We don't know what nationality he is and we sure don't want to cause any immigration problems. What do you say . . . let's go take a look at the boat the kids found him in."

An hour later, Vincent Damar was more baffled than ever. Old wooden sailing ships had been a pet project with him for a long time and he was familiar with the merchant and naval vessels from all the major nations of the world.

Now, after a close examination of the antique construction of the boat the boys had towed home, he was absolutely dumbfounded. "There's no doubt about it . . . this is a longboat, all right, and it's exactly the same type carried by English naval ships for a good eighty years."

"It's not a copy, Dad?"

"Son, you found yourself an original. Even with aged wood, nobody could make a duplicate like this." He pointed to a few spots in the hull. "See there? Boatbuilding details like that have been long lost. Why, they don't even make tools to do it like that now."

"We didn't find it, Dad. That old man did."

Vincent was silent a minute, still studying the boat. "I suppose you noticed what's odd about it, didn't you?"

"No wormholes or barnacles?"

"Exactly. And that boat hasn't been lying up out of water either."

"Vincent . . ."

"Yes, Tim?"

"There are boats in the island that are over a hundred years old."

"But this one is over two hundred and seventy years old."

"It doesn't seem real."

"Dad . . ." Larry said, "you said they carried these longboats *on board* on those naval vessels, didn't you?"

"That's right."

"Could there be . . . could the ship that carried *this* longboat still be in existence?"

"Larry . . . why would you ask that?"

"The name on the transom . . . H.M.S. *Tiger*. It's barely worn at all. Why, the gold leaf is still intact."

"Son . . . there can be reasons that a small boat like this could still be serviceable, but forget about the rest. The *Tiger* . . . the mother ship of this longboat . . . is long since gone."

The silence was long and the boys' eyes watched him carefully. Finally Vincent Damar grinned and said, "Okay, kids, you win. We'll photograph this longboat and send a copy to the British Naval Archives and see what they can come up with on the old ship."

Both the boys let out a loud whoop of pleasure and set about finishing the job of chocking the longboat into place. Timothy looked at Vincent, a broad smile on his face, his teeth flashing white in the sunlight. "I am beginning to think that you have a curious streak too."

"I'm beginning to think those kids can talk me into anything," Vincent retorted with a laugh. "But ... at least it will be fun getting back into some research material again."

"Don't set the Caribbean on its ear, my friend."

"Ha! No way, Timothy. This is nothing more than a wild goose chase."

CHAPTER 2

Eight days after receiving the letter and photographs from Vincent Damar, Sir Harry Arnold, head of the antiquities department of the British Naval Archives, arrived at Peolle Island by helicopter. He carried two bags, one for a small selection of clothes, the other filled with photos, documents, and certain devices for determining the age of wood and metal.

When everyone had been introduced, Sir Harry said, "You have no idea what excitement your photos have caused, Mr. Damar."

"Well, they're not exactly mine, if you recall my letter." He nodded toward his friend Timothy and added, "It was our boys who found the longboat, which was found even earlier by the survivor it carried."

"Ah, yes, and what about that old man?" Sir Harry asked.

"He's better now. Up and beginning to eat well, but we have a communication problem. He speaks a language I don't understand."

"That will make things difficult."

"Not really," Vincent told him. "I sent tapes off to the Language Institute of Miami and we should be hearing from them shortly. So far, they've been able to sort out just about every native tongue and dialect in the entire Caribbean. In one way we're

10

lucky . . . he has some handwritten parchment information on him that he refuses to let anyone see, but I managed to photograph one corner that held a dozen words. At least we're not dealing with some dead language."

"Sir Harry . . ." A pair of youthful faces were looking in the door.

"Yes, Larry?"

"You want to look at the longboat?"

"More than anything you can imagine."

"It's all set up for you on the beach."

"Wonderful. Now we'll see what this is all about."

Sir Harry Arnold was an expert in his work and for the next three hours he went over the longboat, examining every detail inside and out. He measured dimensions and curves, matching them against specifications in an official handbook. Metal and wood underwent chemical tests, and the longer he searched for the identity of the old hull, the more concerned he seemed.

When he finally put down his equipment, he turned and looked at the two fathers with their sons, who had gathered to watch him. "Gentlemen," he said, "as far as I can determine, you have in your possession a genuine, original longboat from His Majesty's Ship *Tiger*, a three-masted naval ship of the line mounting forty-eight guns that was built at the Cremington Boatyards, England, in the year 1791."

"Wow," Josh said softly.

"It's in awfully good condition to be that old," Vincent Damar said doubtfully.

"Nevertheless," Sir Harry insisted, "it is an original. I'm not concerned about *how* it stayed this way . . . I'm simply overjoyed that it did."

"You have any idea how it could have happened, sir?"

Sir Harry nodded. "Possibly, Larry." He paused, looked back at the longboat, and turned around again.

"At the time this boat was built," Sir Harry started, "England had no shortage of lumber. On her shores were some of the finest and longest-lasting woods for a keel, ribs, planking, masts ... anything necessary for a military ship, and fashioning that wood into British ships were the best workmen in the world."

"Wood, once it's cut, is perishable," Vincent told him.

"True, but with limited use and proper attention, it can last a very long time."

"Sir Harry ... in those years British naval vessels certainly weren't in 'limited use' ... in fact, the British navy was the busiest one in the whole world, especially the galleons."

"Correct again, Mr. Damar." Sir Harry smiled and peered at them over his glasses. "However, with the *Tiger* we must make an exception. Her use was *very* limited."

"The *Tiger* never put to sea?" Larry asked hurriedly.

"Oh, she put to sea, all right. In fact, she put to sea twice. The first time was her maiden, shakedown voyage." He paused and smiled again.

Impatiently, Larry and Josh said the same thing at the same time. "What happened?"

"You Americans have a rather strange saying ... yes, ummm, a law. Murphy's Law, I believe you call it."

Larry looked up at his father, frowning.

Vincent told them all, "Murphy's Law states that

no matter what you do, if anything can go wrong, it will." He let out a little laugh at the odd expressions on the faces around him and glanced at Sir Harry. "What's that got to do with the *Tiger?*"

"I'll have to tell the story in my own way," Sir Harry said. "It's a very odd tale, but absolutely true, and I'd be very grateful if you didn't laugh. You see, it has to do with national pride, something we British are quite strong on. And too, there's a degree of superstition involved, plus all the unknowns . . ." He stopped and chuckled. "As I mentioned, it's a very strange story indeed."

Under his breath, Larry told Josh, "If he doesn't get on with it, I'm going to pop!"

"When the keel of the *Tiger* was laid, the Cremington Boatyards were, perhaps, the best in all England. Presiding over the construction of His Majesty's ships was Ashford Hampton, the finest shipwright in the land. He had a force of eighty of the most skilled craftsmen at hand, all well experienced in their work, along with the best materials that could be found. Therefore, you see, no one, not even the king, had any reason to doubt that the *Tiger* would be anything but the finest ship afloat.

"I imagine that it was Ashford Hampton himself who felt the twinges of doubt first. Chocks would slip, tools would break, exactly measured parts refused to fit into place. At first, it was little things, annoying things, but as those were overcome, bigger, more irritating things began to happen.

"The Cremington Boatyards had always prided themselves on being able to adhere to a schedule, but with the *Tiger* . . . well, this was a different matter entirely. They began to fall behind, first by days, then weeks and months. Ashford Hampton even put on more men, but that didn't help either.

"Finally, six months behind time, the hull was finished and the *Tiger* was ready to be floated and finished while moored to the main dock. That was when the first workman was injured. After that there was one injury after another, and now they were calling the *Tiger* a jinx ship. Everyone was afraid to work on her, and if it hadn't been for Ashford Hampton they all would have left the project. Somehow he appealed to their pride and they kept on the job ... but one thing they kept to themselves was the fact that they considered the *Tiger* to be carrying a built-in jinx it would never lose, and anyone sailing on her would have nothing but bad luck.

"Now, at this time, England was the greatest naval power in the world, and she needed ships, ships, and more ships. The king himself grew insistent that the *Tiger* be finished, and despite the fear of the jinx, they hurried the job, and at long last she was done and fitted, guns installed, and a crew drawn to man her. Oh, it was a great day when she sailed downstream to the mouth of the river and headed out to sea. It was to be a journey of three months to make sure all was in proper working order. Then the *Tiger* would put back to port for a fresh supply of water and food, get her sailing orders, and be off to some foreign lands."

For a moment, Sir Harry paused, scowling off into the distance. "That maiden voyage only took one month," he said. "It was the worst month in England's history. Abroad, there was nothing but trouble, our ships running into difficulty no matter where they were. In England itself there were great fires and some strange disease that put a quarter of the population in their beds ... and that was when those men who worked on the *Tiger* mentioned the jinx ship.

"That being a time when believing in superstition was common, you can imagine how the people reacted. The story spread like wildfire until all England was blaming everything that went wrong on the ship the king had sent to sea. In fact, it got so bad that mobs were forming to force the king to send out a squadron of ships to find and sink the *Tiger*!

"Well, he never had to do that, because one day the sails of that jinx ship showed on the horizon, and in came the *Tiger*, her canvas storm-ripped, her crew sick, the captain in his bunk with a broken leg, and a bandaged first officer at the helm.

"There was no noise, no shouting and whistling to welcome her back. There was just a deadly, wide-eyed quiet, with everybody too afraid to speak. When the injured were taken off, the shipyard crew went back on board to survey the damage and couldn't believe what they found. Cannons had split open on their first round. Some had lasted longer, then blown up. The water casks had sprung leaks and all the crew had to drink was rainwater they managed to save. Food had spoiled, water seemed to come into the hull from every seam, and they had to work the pumps constantly to keep the ship afloat. Even the weather went against them. A small squall that never should have bothered them a bit ripped their sails apart.

"My story about the *Tiger* hinges on what happened next. From the minute they took the ship out of action, everything seemed to change. There were no more fires, the sick got better, news from other areas improved, and now all of England seemed to know something special.

"It was the jinx ship that had caused all the trouble! The delegation from the city didn't have any trouble getting their petition before the king, or having him sign it. You see, the king was one of those who got sick too, and a nearby fire had almost spread to the palace itself. In fact, as much as he needed ships, he was glad to get this one off his hands.

"The only trouble was how they were going to do it. Nobody wanted to dismantle a jinx ship, and burning it could be dangerous. It was Ashford Hampton who came up with the final idea. You see, he didn't believe in this superstition business one bit, and being a lover of fine boats, he didn't want to see this one destroyed ... especially now, since not one thing had happened to her the past two weeks at the dock. There was no more leakage, the water casks were holding fine, and the new casks and cannon they had installed made the *Tiger* a proud beauty indeed ... but not a beauty the people wanted in their city.

"So ... because they were afraid to offend the jinx that inhabited her, Ashford Hampton and a small crew took her down the river again, set the sails with her prow headed out to sea, lashed the wheel in position, and climbed over the side to their pilot boat. From there they watched the *Tiger* sail west to an unknown fate, fully provisioned, armed to the teeth, a brand-new fighting ship of the line sailing into a setting sun with a ghost crew on a journey no one would ever record in a logbook."

Slowly, Sir Harry turned and looked at the longboat nestling in its chocks. "Until this moment, gentlemen, the *Tiger* had never been heard from. It was assumed that she had succumbed to the elements and sunk."

Vincent Damar caught Sir Harry's attention. "She *could* have sunk. It isn't unusual for ship's boats to float loose from a sinking ship."

Sir Harry shook his head. "Are you familiar with the old shipboard practices of the British navy?"

"No, sir. I never got into those details."

"Let me tell you then . . . the way the longboats were lashed down, there was no way they would have come loose accidentally." He smiled and said, "But we're back to Murphy's Law again, aren't we?"

"How's that?"

"Whatever could go wrong did. We have the *Tiger's* longboat right here with us." There was not much they could add to that, so they just looked at each other and shrugged. "Now . . . there is one thing you could do." He looked at the two boys and went on. "You can sell this boat back to the British government. It would make an excellent museum piece."

"It isn't ours," Larry stated. "You'll have to ask him . . . but what can he say? Nobody understands him."

Sir Harry smiled and put his arms around the boys' shoulders. "Well, there's always sign language. What say we go in and speak to the old gent?"

As he watched the three of them go toward the house, Timothy flashed his teeth in a broad, white smile and said, "Vincent, my friend, I have a feeling that your wild goose chase is getting a good start."

Vincent didn't answer him. He was beginning to get that same feeling too.

In Miami Beach, one block east of Biscayne Boulevard on the fifth floor of the Wallace Building, three men were seated at one end of a conference table, intent upon the voices coming from the tape recorder in front of them. The one operating the machine was short and balding, his skin tanned from the Florida sun. Behind his glasses his eyes were narrow and shifty, greed set deep inside them.

At first glance, the other pair seemed to be well-dressed businessmen, but there was something different about them. For one thing, neither was burned from the sun, and their clothes seemed strangely out of date. Both of them were big, with wide shoulders and powerful hands. The one called Aktur Cilon had a fine red scar down his left cheek, while his friend, Embor Linero, had the first joint of his right pinky finger missing.

When the tape ended, associate language director Herbert Mackley turned off the switch, leaned back, and looked at the two men across from him. "Are you satisfied?" he asked.

"How do we know that the recording is authentic?"

"Since when has that language been in use?" Mackley demanded.

"*You* knew it," Embor said pointedly.

Mackley shook his head. "Not like that. Nobody on the outside can speak it like that. All I did was recognize it. Oh, I understand it, all right, but you know as well as I do *nobody* can speak it anymore."

"That person on your tape can."

The crafty smile that crossed Mackley's face said a lot. "Exactly, gentlemen, and as hard as your government tried, it wasn't able to erase the original language of the country of Grandau after all. Over two hundred and fifty years, and it's still there in its original purity."

Aktur shrugged. "After all, Mr. Mackley, it is still only a recording."

Mackley knew he had them then. Deliberately,

he poured himself a drink of water, took his time about finishing it, then put the glass down and made wet rings on the tabletop. "Your new country has always been in a state of unrest. The people give you nothing but trouble and you know as well as I do that if they decide to get from under the control of your government, there is no way you can stop them."

"I doubt that," Embor Linero said firmly.

Mackley smiled, a hard, nasty smile. "Even if a descendant of their good King Tynere suddenly appeared with positive documents to show he is the true heir to the crown? You forget . . . the nation of Grandau was a free, wealthy, and happy place until your ancestors grew jealous and ran an army through them and stripped them of all their possessions."

"They were weak," Embor said.

"They were ambushed," Mackley told him. "Now they have a chance to get back at you people."

Both the men knew the time for talk had ended. Embor Linero leaned forward, his hands folded on the tabletop. "How much will it cost us to know where this tape came from?"

"One million dollars," Mackley said evenly.

"That is a lot of money."

Mackley shrugged. "That is a lot of information. After all, you are paying for . . . the elimination of certain people."

"Quite right," Embor said. "Now, shall we do business?"

The associate director of languages of the institute nodded and began to lay out his demands. The tape recording itself didn't mean a thing. It was the letter giving Vincent Damar's address that was valuable. And now he had to act quickly before Vincent

Damar got impatient and possibly contacted another language expert.

An hour later the arrangements had been made. Herbert Mackley was taking no chances on having Aktur or Embor eliminate *him,* so that when the money was put in the bank under *his* name and the passbook was left with the head cashier (who would verify the transaction by phone and hold it until told where to send it), only then would the two men be given the name and address of Vincent Damar.

They left the building at ten-minute intervals, then Aktur Cilon and Embor Linero met in a small foreign restaurant. After coffee Aktur said, "Will it be easy to handle the man Mackley?"

His friend nodded. "Certainly. He is a fool."

"And the others?"

Embor's shrug was eloquent. "Simple. We do as our ancestors did to the people of Grandau ... we ambush them."

CHAPTER 3

The small group in Vincent Damar's house on Peolle Island were gathered around the old man who was sitting smiling in the rocker, for the first time able to communicate with his new friends.

"You did a great job, Sir Harry."

"Simple sign language to start with," he told Vincent. "We may not be able to *write* his language at present, but we know how to match words and objects now. At least we know his name . . . Vali Steptur, and by finger count he is seventy-two years old."

Supper was a laughing time with everyone trying to add to the conversation. Before it was over Vali had managed to convey to them with a pencil drawing that he had come from another island in the southern chain and the number of people on it amounted to forty-six. He drew a lot more stick figures and showed with gestures that at one time in the past there had been a great deal more of them. But he rocked in his chair to indicate an earthquake and blew hard at the paper with one finger pointing toward the sky to mimic a great storm, then ran the pencil through most of the drawn figures to show how many had been lost.

It was Larry who finally got a sense of distance

through to Vali, pointing first to his island, then to the others, and looking curiously at the old man.

Vali's face tightened and he looked scared. Slowly, he shook his head in the universal language that meant "no." Then carefully, he took the pencil and drew another picture. It wasn't a stick figure this time. It was rough, but a lot of detail went into it, and when he was done he turned it around.

"What do you suppose that is?" Sir Harry asked.

Only a few seconds were spent studying the sketch, then Vincent nodded with understanding. "It's a young girl."

"But there's something important about it, isn't there?"

"There certainly is," Vincent told him. "She's wearing a crown on her head."

The old man knew that his message had been understood. Then, with a simple gesture, he took the leather folder from his lap and passed it to Vincent.

There was no need for Vali to tell him exactly how valuable his treasure was. The fine lambskin parchment so beautifully decorated with artwork, inscribed with magnificent penmanship, and stamped with an aged waxen seal that fixed red, blue, and gold ribbons to the document said it all.

Something else was in the folder too, carefully wrapped in old yellowed linen. When Vincent unwrapped it, a magnificent gold ring, faced with a royal crest and surrounded by diamonds, dropped into his palm.

And now, Vincent Damar didn't have to wonder about his guest any longer. His research into the histories of European countries had supplied him with everything he needed to know. Pictures of that crest on the ring were well known to students of the times and events that turned Europe upside down those many years ago.

"What is it, Dad?"

His dad held the ring up in his fingers for all to see. "This is the royal seal of the nation of Grandau that was crushed by an oppressor nation when Tynere was its king."

He looked at Vali, saw his shining eyes because the old man recognized the name of his country and king, then everything made sense. "Sir Harry," he said, "I think we have something of international importance here."

The Englishman said nothing, his face serious.

"It's more than just a longboat from the *Tiger* now." He rewrapped the ring and put it back in the folder. "If I'm not missing my guess, on Vali's island are the heirs to the throne of Grandau and these are the documents to prove it."

Sir Harry seemed confused. "But Mr. Damar . . . how could they possibly have gotten there?"

This time it was Vincent's turn to tell a story. Carefully, he sorted out the facts in his mind, then said, "When Grandau was overrun by that neighboring country, certain members of the royal family and their servants managed to escape. They got to the coastline with the enemy in hot pursuit and purchased an old fishing boat to take them to safety in England. They never arrived. Folklore has it that the boat left the harbor hours before their pursuers showed up, but there was no chase after that since a vicious storm came up that would have put such a small boat in terrible danger. As far as the enemy was concerned, that small band of people were as good as dead, and they went back and reported it that way. Afterwards, there was no longer any royal family to rule over Grandau. Since that time there has been nothing but one dictatorship after another."

"Yes, Mr. Damar, that puts them off the European coast in a small, ill-equipped, and rickety boat, but not here in the Caribbean."

"There is one thing here that fits both pictures, Sir Harry."

"Oh, and what is that?"

"The *Tiger*'s longboat."

"Certainly . . . you don't mean . . ."

"Yes, I do mean, Sir Harry. It's quite possible that the storm drove that small boat out to sea, and no doubt that eventually it would have foundered and sunk, but before it did another ship came by at exactly the right time, a fully equipped, brand-new ship with no captain, no crew, and no place to go at all."

"The H.M.S. *Tiger!*"

"Right."

"But . . . those were people from inland, not seafarers!"

"I don't think they cared much. The *Tiger* was there, they went aboard, and they just let it sail. The trade winds did the rest. They blew them right smack into the Caribbean and they've been here ever since. On some island south of Peolle, probably in the Cardiff Chain, are an ancient people speaking an ancient language no longer in use, and in their midst is a young girl, a princess to the crown of Grandau."

Larry glanced up at his dad, a thoughtful expression on his face. "Would it make any difference if they got back to their home in Europe?"

"Son . . . that's a strange section of the world. They have long memories and they have never given up hope of becoming an independent kingdom again."

"But now that neighboring country controls the whole area."

"No matter . . . if Grandau was independent again, or had a reason to rebel, it is so strategically placed that it could cause more trouble than it's worth. Frankly, I think they'd simply let Grandau alone if a descendant of King Tynere showed up, but if they found out about the heir ahead of time, they'd do everything in their power to destroy what is left of those original survivors."

"Well then, Mr. Damar, that should be no trouble. Apparently no one but us knows of their existence."

Vincent frowned and gnawed at his lip. "That may not be so, Sir Harry. It all depends on what Vali here said on those tapes when he was trying to make himself known to me."

"But I'm certain the Language Institute is reliable."

"No doubt, but greed can do strange things to people. Let's hope that everyone at the institute is honest."

Until now, Josh had been silent. Finally he said, "There is one thing we do not know. The stories you tell are great adventures, but one thing is missing."

"What's that, Josh?" Vincent asked.

"What happened to the *Tiger*?"

"Yes," Sir Harry stated. "What *did* happen to her, do you suppose?"

"Can I guess?"

"Of course."

"The *Tiger* probably grounded off that island and the passengers let the longboat down and rowed to shore. They might even have had time to take off enough supplies to get them started in a new life before the tides and wind floated the *Tiger* off to some burial spot in the ocean. Until Vali here used it, that longboat has been in their hands."

"I'm glad you're guessing, Dad," Larry said.

"Why?"

"Because it's not the way I'd guess."

Vincent smiled at his friend Timothy and then he looked back at his son. "Then how would *you* guess?"

Larry let his eyes watch Sir Harry intently. "Remember . . . you said the *Tiger* was a jinx ship?"

"Well, that was what they called her *then*. Of course, with the strange things that happened to her, they had reason to."

"She wasn't a jinx ship, Sir Harry," Larry told him. "I think the *Tiger* was a special ship. She didn't want to go to war or police the seas. She had one special job to do and she was determined to do it." He paused, then said firmly, "I think the *Tiger* knew the reason it was built was to rescue the royal family of Grandau, and right now it's waiting to finish its job."

The envelope was delivered to the hotel suite of Aktur Cilon and Embor Linero in the afternoon mail and when they opened it they found a photocopy of Vincent Damar's original letter to the Language Institute of Miami. Aktur read it carefully, got out a small book of maps, and opened it to the Caribbean sea. He studied it a moment, then circled a small spot with his pencil. "Here," he said. "Peolle Island."

"How far from the mainland?" Embor queried.

"There is no airfield indicated, so if we fly it would be by helicopter and I would estimate a four-hour trip."

"A helicopter would alert them, I'm afraid. We would do better to hire a boat."

"That is a problem too," Aktur replied. "Those boat captains stay on the radio. The answer is, I think, an outright purchase of a sailing boat. It will be no trouble to fake a breakdown and give us a good reason for landing on Peolle."

"Excellent, comrade. At least this will be a pleasurable assignment for us. At home they will be buried in snow and here we are warm and comfortable with a nice sea voyage coming up. It makes, ah, eliminating the others a real pleasure."

"Embor ... we can make this assignment even more pleasurable if we wish to."

"Oh? And how would that be?"

"Our government has given us the million dollars for the purchase of this information from the man Mackley, has it not?"

"Yes, that is true."

"It expects no return, does it?"

"The information and elimination is worth much more than a million dollars to them," Embor said.

Aktur Cilon smiled grimly. "Then if we take back the million dollars from Mackley and eliminate him too, our government would think nothing of it, would they?"

With a conspiratorial grin, Embor nodded. "Not as long as they knew nothing of it. But tell me, comrade, where will we spend all that money?"

"Simplicity itself, my friend. We do just like so many others. We just disappear at sea after our final report to headquarters when the elimination is accomplished. They will think we perished at sea and will never realize that we have become part of the great population of the United States."

"You know, comrade," Embor said, "you are more clever than I ever thought. If nothing goes wrong, we can spend the rest of our lives in absolute splendor."

Aktur Cilon laughed humorlessly. "Comrade ... what could go wrong? We are dealing with nothing but simple islanders and a schoolteacher and a couple of kids. What trouble could *they* cause?"

Everything was an exciting surprise to old Vali Steptur, from photos in the books and albums to the shortwave radio on the shelf. But he was an intelligent man and these things came easily to him. Many times he had seen the faraway specks of sailing ships on the horizon and occasionally airplanes would go by overhead, leaving long thin cloudlike forms behind them. Often, he had known there was another world outside that on the island they had named Halu, but it was a world they were all afraid of.

For generations they had let it be thought that Halu was totally uninhabited, shielding their fires and living in hand-built houses that looked exactly like the rest of the landscape unless you were standing right on top of them.

They had always been a proud people and smart, keeping their heritage intact, everyone being able to read, write, and count. From mouth to mouth the story of Grandau and the escape from the enemy had been handed down without any detail being lost, and always they had planned for the day when they would return.

But that day never seemed to come. The prince that had come in the original party had married and had had a son, and in time that son had married too, his wife giving him a daughter. With each generation, the royal house had been preserved, the lineage kept on a hidden scroll for future use ...

and even now on Halu, there was a royal princess, heir to the throne of Grandau.

Vali Steptur's ancestor had been the teacher and good friend of King Tynere. He had given his pledge to the king to protect the prince, even with his life if need be. That pledge had been handed down from father to son throughout the generations, and now it rested in Vali's hands.

And after all this time, it was Vali Steptur who knew that if something didn't happen shortly, there never would be a return to Grandau; so as the sea brought them there, he let the sea bring them back. He found the secret place they all thought was only a silly legend, pulled the longboat out into the sun, then filled the water cask and shoved off with the leather folder under his arm to prove his story.

Looking back toward Halu Island, he could see the dark shadow of the opening in the cliff. It had been dark and scary in there. He knew there was something else there too. It was a huge, awesome thing, a deadly menace that seemed to be waiting there, ready to pounce. He shook the idea out of his head. He was getting old. What he saw was probably nothing more than shadows in that enormous cave.

Now he knew that he had made the right move. He had found friends, true friends among these strange people. They had taken care of him, fed him, and now they were actually able to talk to each other, even if most of the talk was with signs or drawn pictures. When the white-haired man who was so interested in his old boat showed him the pictures of that same boat in a large book and indicated what he wanted, Vali laughed and showed that he understood by pointing to the longboat and making a gesture of giving it to him.

He didn't quite understand why they seemed so happy about it, but the white-haired man waited for the other to do something to the machine-that-talked on the shelf, then he spoke into the funny block tied by a coiled string to the main machine.

What Sir Harry was doing was contacting Miami on the shortwave radio, and when he got Kevin Smith he said into the microphone, "Harry Arnold here, old boy. Good news ... the longboat was authentic."

The voice from the speaker said, "Wonderful! Have you been able to buy it?"

"I'm afraid not, old chap."

"Oh, no." The voice was totally dejected.

Sir Harry laughed. "Don't worry, chap. The owner gave it to me. As soon as we make arrangements, it will be on board a freighter and into the British Museum."

"And ... it was from the *Tiger*?"

"No doubt about it, Kevin. The original longboat."

"I wonder what really did happen to the old lady."

"Well, I'm afraid we'll never know about that, but at least we have part of her. Can you get one of the interisland boats to make a stop by here as soon as possible?"

"Right, Harry. The *Gull* is in port now. I'll contact the captain and he should make the pickup by Wednesday. Will you be coming back with the longboat?"

"Old boy, after all this, there's no way I'm going to let it out of my sight until I see it safely in the museum. By the way, I have a great story to tell you in connection with the *Tiger*. Probably all legend and speculation, but mighty interesting. And too ... it could be true, you know."

* * *

Aktur Cilon handed the briefcase to his partner and let him examine the packages of money that were stacked so neatly inside. "A million dollars," he mused. "Was it difficult?"

"The man Mackley was in too much of a hurry. I knew he would not be able to wait very long before taking the money out of the bank. He would want it where it would be out of sight of the tax men. It was a simple matter."

"He is, ah . . . eliminated?"

"Permanently," Aktur said.

"Then shall we look into the matter of obtaining ourselves a boat and learn the ways of rich men before we finish our assignment?"

"Excellent thought, comrade. It shall be business with pleasure and no need to hurry at all. Those people have been here over two hundred years and I am sure a few days or weeks longer will not matter at all."

"There is a small problem, however."

"And what is that?"

"This schoolteacher . . . Vincent Damar," Embor said. "Supposing he does not believe that letter we sent him?"

"Why shouldn't he? It was on the stationery of the Language Institute with Mackley's signature at the bottom. It was a clever forgery."

"I mean the contents . . . he may not believe it."

"Nonsense. He asked for the origin of the language and we told him the truth. The message was very simple, just the plea of an old man looking for help, that his boat had been wrecked and his papers were old family documents that he fancied. Besides, what would an island schoolteacher care about it anyway? All he probably wanted was to shove the old man off on some government agency to take

care of him. Anyway, we'll have them all eliminated before he knows what has happened."

On Wednesday morning the interisland steamer
dropped off the mail and hoisted the longboat from
the H.M.S. *Tiger* on board. From the dock the small
group waved at the departing figure of Sir Harry
Arnold until he was out of sight.

Only then did Vincent Damar open his letter and
read it. Something in his face made Larry ask,
"Bad news, Dad?"

"No, just puzzling."

Larry saw the postmark on the envelope. "The
institute couldn't figure it out?"

His father handed him the letter. "Apparently
they did. It just doesn't seem to tie in somehow."

When he finished, Larry handed the letter back.
"Dad . . . if the old man was on *another* boat, he
could have told us that when he was drawing those
pictures."

"I know."

"Would he lie to us?"

"Son, I sure don't think so."

"Then why . . ."

"It's an old language, son, a dialect that hasn't
been spoken in the civilized world for a couple of
hundred years. It wouldn't be hard for a translator
to make a mistake at all."

"You don't think that, do you, Dad?"

"Right now I don't know what to think. Let's go
take Vali back to the drawing board again. If he
can sketch an outline of his island, maybe we can
find someone who can recognize it."

It took fifteen minutes to get the idea across to
the old man, but when he knew what they were
after, he went at it eagerly, sketching Halu from
several different directions, indicated by the posi-

tion of a model sun in the sky. When he finally decided that he could do no more, he handed the paper to Vincent.

Knowing he wasn't that experienced in the islands, he let Timothy take a look at it. And Timothy *was* experienced. He looked up, puzzled. "This is Montique Island, Vincent."

Quickly, Vincent found it on the map. "The southernmost in the Cardiff Chain."

"But something's wrong, my friend."

"What's wrong?"

"No one lives there," Timothy told him. "There is no water, nothing will grow, and to the islanders it is only a place of the old dead. They will not go near it."

"So that is why they have never been discovered," Vincent half whispered to himself. "How long will it take to get there by boat?"

"Three days by sail," Timothy said, "if the winds blow well and there are no storms to fight."

"Day cruising only?"

Timothy nodded. "It is better to anchor in a cove at night."

"Okay," Vincent decided, "I'll start outfitting the *Blue Tuna II* in the morning. We'll get two weeks' supplies on board, have the depth finder fixed, and go see what this is all about."

"Dad . . ."

"What, son?"

"You'll be a week getting the *Blue Tuna* ready again."

"I know, but there's no way to shorten the time. Why?"

"Josh and I have the *Sea Eagle* all ready. We could go ahead and you could follow when you're outfitted."

With an annoyed tone of voice Vincent said, "Son, that's a three-day trip. I can't let you two kids . . ." Then he stopped and grinned slightly. "I keep telling you the same thing, don't I?"

"That's okay, Dad."

"Sorry, son. I just keep forgetting that you two keep growing up. You sure you can handle a voyage like this?"

"Remember our trip to the Shrinking Island?" Larry reminded him.

"How can I forget it?" He glanced over at Timothy. "Is it all right with you?"

"Island boys must learn the ways of the sea early," Timothy said, looking at his son fondly.

"Okay," Vincent agreed. "When do you want to get started?" Before the kids could answer he cut in, "Yeah, I know, right now." He let out a laugh and handed them the charts they would need. "Go plot your course, get your gear aboard, and move on out."

Larry gave him a big grin and a hug. "You're great, Dad."

On the other side of the room, Josh was doing the same to his father.

By the time the sun was centered over Peolle, the *Sea Eagle* was out of sight. Idly, Vincent picked up the Miami paper that had been dropped off by the interisland steamer. He flipped the pages, looking at the two-day-old news, then he paused at an item and frowned.

Timothy saw the look on his face and said, "Are you troubled, my friend?"

"I don't know." He reached in his pocket and took out the letter from the Language Institute of Miami. He checked the names and put the letter back. "Timothy, something is *very* wrong. I've received a letter written by a man a day after the police found his body in a mangrove swamp."

"But . . . that's impossible."

"Exactly, but Herbert Mackley, the man I sent the tape of Vali Steptur's voice, was found murdered."

"Who would do such a thing, Vincent?"

Seriously, Vincent said, "Someone who knows the true importance of the survivors of Grandau nobility . . . and the trouble they could make for a modern dictatorship."

"Then they'll be looking for Halu . . . or Montique Island too."

"I'm afraid so."

"We should recall the boys."

"There's no way now, Timothy. They won't be wasting the battery charge listening in all day. We'll have to get them at sundown when we planned the contact."

"We must trust that the boys can take care of themselves then."

"They always have," Vincent said.

But in his heart, Vincent was scared. They were only boys, half grown and adventurous.

There were others who were killers.

Vincent Damar wasn't going to take any chances. He flipped the switch on the radio to the ON position, let it warm up, then tuned in the frequency of his friend's marina on the Florida keys. He gave the call letters three times, then a crisp voice repeated them with "Herman's Marina Service, can I help you?"

"Hi, Herm. It's Vincent Damar."

"Good to hear from you. What's up?"

"I need some information. Did you see where a man named Herbert Mackley from the Language

Institute was found dead? The police think he was murdered."

"Yeah, Vince, I saw that. It's in today's paper again too."

"Really? What's it say?"

There was a crackle of static, then Herman said, "Just an item of how the police have his suspected killers in custody. They were two escaped convicts hiding out in the swamp."

"They say what Mackley was doing there?"

"Sure. He had rented a boat and a shack out on one of those islands. He had plenty of provisions . . . fishing equipment and all that, so apparently he was going to take a good vacation." He paused, then added, "He just picked the wrong spot. Those convicts had been on the loose for ten days when Mackley turned up with the perfect answer for their escape . . . a boat and plenty of food and clothing. Hey . . . what's all this about?"

"Mackley was somebody I wrote to, that's all."

"Well, if I can help any other way, just let me know. When are you bringing the *Blue Tuna II* for the valve job on the port engine?"

"Next month, Herm. See you then."

"Roger and out, Vince."

Timothy had overheard the whole conversation and saw the relief in his friend's face. "Feel better now?"

"Much," Vincent told him. "At least we don't have to get the International Patrol Squadron out to chase the kids down."

Forty miles away, the two men in the sailing sloop *Dragonfish* had given up trying to navigate against the wind. They had begun to realize that even in a calm sea with a gentle wind, there was more to handling a boat than they had thought.

Aktur Cilon had gotten disgusted with their progress, so he and his partner lowered the mainsail and jib, let them lie in a sloppy pile on the deck, and Aktur started the small diesel engine. Now there was no trouble at all. He simply followed a compass course and enjoyed the day while he could. Peolle Island and those to be eliminated were only a short way off. On their starboard side was the outline of a power cruiser. One of the island boats, Aktur suspected.

Had he been closer, or used his binoculars, he could have read the name on its transom ... the *Blue Tuna II*. Of course, he wouldn't have known it was heading north to Ara Island for a full refitting and on board were the targets of his planned "elimination."

CHAPTER 4

For the boys, the first day out had been filled with the exciting planning of their visit to Montique Island, or, as Vali had called it, "Halu." At their first landfall, the islanders of Peke had come down to greet them, roasted many fish in their honor, and sat by the fire the early part of the night to tell them about Montique.

None of them had ever been there, or even planned to go. As far as they knew, it was a barren place without water or plant life, unhospitable and of no use at all. However, they wished the boys luck before they left, certain they would find nothing more than they had been told.

Just as the last embers of the fire were going out, Josh asked, "What do you think about Montique Island, Larry?"

"I think Dad was right," Larry answered. "If the old man *did* come from there, then there has to be water and vegetation. All these islands are volcanic in origin, and there could possibly be a bowl inside the rim of Montique nobody knows about."

"The islanders have been here a long time."

"Yes, I know, but they have their own legends. If their ancestors said it's an empty island, then they say it too and pass it down to their kids. So who wants to go to an empty island anyway? They have everything they need or want right here."

Josh nodded in agreement. "I guess you're right." He looked across the fire at his friend. "What will we do if it is empty?"

"Old Vali Steptur came from somewhere."

"Maybe it wasn't Montique Island."

"The pictures he drew of it sure looked like it. Your father has even been around it and he said it was Montique, all right."

"Well, pal, we'll sure find out pretty soon, won't we?"

"One way or the other. Good night, Josh."

" 'Night, Larry."

Montique Island seemed to simply grow out of the sea like a giant barnacle. Its sides were irregular craggy cliffs and there was no place to make a landing except on the southeast quadrant, where a small white beach glistened in the brilliant sunlight. Behind the beach were a few scraggly palms struggling for existence in the sands before the slope edged upward at a lesser angle, the dull face of the rock etched by the winds of time.

To all the world, Montique was nothing but a rock, a great barren rock not worth climbing because nothing would be at the top anyway. But the world could be wrong.

At the very peak, behind a barricade of flat stones, two men were peering through an ancient brass telescope at the sailboat that had just dropped anchor off their island. The sun had burned them brown, but they weren't like the other islanders at all. Their hair was light and their eyes combinations of blue and brown, their manner of speech not at all like that of anyone else in the world.

"What do you see, Jon?"

The man with the telescope extended it for a better focus, studied the boat a minute, then said, "Two boys, Georg. No one else."

"What could they want?"

Jon shrugged. "Who knows what any boys want? At least they are alone."

"That could be bad."

"Why, Georg?"

"Because there is no grown person there to control them. They might want to explore."

"Nonsense. Even boys would know it is too dangerous to try to climb up here."

"Jon . . . they *could* find the way. It wouldn't be hard if they really looked."

"Why should they?" his friend asked. "There is nothing here for them to look for."

Georg was quiet a few moments, thinking. "Possibly Vali . . ."

"Vali is dead, my friend. He was an old man. He never could have survived out there alone. We tried to tell him, but he wouldn't listen. For too many years he had been dreaming about returning to put Tila on the throne of Grandau and it was too much for him."

"We should have stopped him."

Jon laid his hand on Georg's shoulder and shook his head. "We never even knew he left. Oh, sure, he talked about looking for the secret place hidden here on Halu where our ancestors were supposed to have provided a way for us, but we know such a place is only a story that old men tell children by the fires at night. There never was such a place, Georg. Old Vali must have roped those logs together that we saw on the beach and floated away on them."

"He took the king's papers and the Great Ring," Georg remarked sadly. "They can never be replaced. Now we have no proof any longer. The throne is not Tila's now."

"You worry too much, Georg. The proof will be found. Somewhere, somehow, we will find it." Jon picked up the telescope and centered it on the anchored boat again. For a moment he watched the boys, then said, "They are blowing air into one of those funny soft boats like we found on the beach that time."

"A very poor boat. When I touched a knife to it the wind whistled out and it went flat. Whoever heard of making a boat out of cloth like that?"

"It is the ways of these water people, Georg. Remember, we are from Grandau; we must make ourselves remember that. Our place is far across this ocean."

"Too many generations have passed, Jon. There is no memory, only words and stories. The only land we really know is right here. There was a time when we almost did leave this island because we had to. There were just too many of us . . . then the earth shook and half the people died. When that terrible storm covered this place, even more went. I remember that . . . I was just a child then, but I remember that. Now we are just a few."

But Jon was hardly listening. His eye was glued to the telescope and he said, "They are paddling this way." A few minutes later he folded the telescope shut and stood up. "They've landed on the beach. I think we should go tell the others. In case they decide to look around this island, we must be ready to discourage their efforts."

*   *   *

It would never change, Tila thought, *whenever an outsider appeared near their island, you could see the fear on their faces.* They protected her like a girl ... in fact, a young lady ... and except for the few boys and girls on the island, she had never seen anyone else her own age.

And now there were two of them below on the beach and neither Jon nor Georg would let her go near the rim. Even Helena and Margo were firm about it, their hands trembling, eyes darting about like a bird when a cat was near. It was a little annoying to be protected from *everything*. Why, when she was little they wouldn't even let her pick up a bug, and she was nine before they allowed her to feel the sand under her toes and the sea licking at her legs. Oh, they didn't just *let* her do those things ... she had to insist upon it, and then she didn't realize that she was a princess, heir to the vacant throne of Grandau. Sometimes she wondered where Grandau was. As far as she was concerned, the island they called Halu *was* the world. From the topmost part of it, all that could be seen was the deep blue-green of the sea.

The blood of that ancient King Tynere that flowed through her veins suddenly stiffened and Tila stood there flat-footed, legs spread apart, her hands on her hips. "You ... Helena and Margo," she demanded. "Am I your princess?"

"Oh, yes!"

"Tila ... of course you are!" Both women spoke as one.

"Very well. In that case I insist on being shown those who have come to our shore!"

"But, Tila ..."

She didn't flinch. She simply stood her ground

and looked at them sternly. It was the first time since her parents had died that this royal tone had been used, and once again they understood why the old ones had been so careful in marrying and having children to inherit the crown of a nation.

A word was spoken to the men, and while the others stayed back, Jon and Georg escorted Tila to the viewing place. Jon opened the telescope and handed it to her.

Tila's hands were shaking so hard she had to draw a deep breath, then let it out slowly so she could see through the glass. For the first time in her life, she was about to see someone she hadn't known since she had been born.

When they finished eating, Josh raked dead ashes over the glowing coals to bank the fire and have it ready for later. Larry had cleaned up the metal utensils, stacked them away in the box, and now he was surveying the sloping face of the cliff behind the beach.

The area they were on was as long as three football fields, the sand littered with dried driftwood. White ghost crabs poked their eyes out of their sand holes, made sure they were safe, then hurled a clawful of dirt into a ring around their nests. The birds that had flown off when they first landed had come back to dig tiny coquina clams out of the sand, then chased the waves back and forth, picking at the bottom for other minute sea creatures.

Josh came over and stood by his friend. "See anything?"

"Just rock."

"You must learn to see more when you look," Josh said.

"Oh?"

"It is rock that has been used, Larry." He pointed to a dark streak to his left. "See there, the line that goes up between the two boulders?"

When his eyes found it, Larry nodded.

"That is an old path."

"You've got eyes like a hawk," Larry said. "I would never have known that. How do you know it's an old one?"

"The color." Josh showed him. "If it were used more often it would be lighter."

"Who would use it?"

Josh didn't say anything. He tilted his head back and half closed his eyes. Larry saw his nostrils move gently and he knew what Josh was doing. Finally Josh asked, "Do you smell it?"

"Pal, all I smell is the ocean and some smoke from our fire. What are you talking about?"

"There is a smell of green things, Larry. It is more than the sea smells. It is like the garden behind my cousin's house when everything is almost ripe enough to pick."

"Where can there be any green things, Josh? Good golly, this place is all rock."

Josh pointed at the motion on top of a flat area partway up the slope. "What do you call that?"

"Birds," Larry said.

"There is something special about them. Just look close."

Then Larry let out a long, low whistle, and envied Josh's knowledge of the things of the wild. They were birds, all right, but they weren't seabirds at all. They were what the natives called *dekkies* and were only native to land areas where they could feed on seeds and nuts.

"You're right, Josh. There's green foliage around here and most likely on top ... and if there is green vegetation, that means there is water too ... so there could very well be people."

"I'm quite sure of it," Josh stated emphatically.

When Larry looked, Josh was smiling gently. "Why?"

"If you look at the top of the rim very carefully, you may see something."

Larry raised his eyes and searched the rocky lip above him. He had to scan the entire area twice, then he saw it. Up there a pinpoint of light reflected brightly off polished metal, and when he raised his head to study it more closely, it disappeared.

"You see it?"

Larry bobbed his head. "Somebody is watching us through a spyglass!"

"Exactly, and we don't want to disturb them."

"You're right, Josh. Tonight we'll just sack out by the fire here, and tomorrow, after they see that we're friendly, we'll find the way up there."

They should never have worried about that. Whatever went around their faces, whatever unguent was in that cloth held to their noses made everything dreamlike, and when they awoke their hands and feet were tightly bound, their heads a throbbing ball of pain. And when they looked up, framed in the only light they could see was the black shadow of some monstrous creature that babbled wild sounds, and both the boys moaned in total despair.

Jon stared down at the two figures at his feet and said to Georg, "Now we have stooped to capturing children."

"Those *children*, as you call them, have sailed a ship to our shores."

"I don't think they were trying to destroy us."

"You saw them watching us up here."

"That was an accident."

"Our princess's life was at stake!"

"My friend," Jon said, "always I have been accused of being the hotheaded one, always ready to do the foolish thing. Now you have led us to this mad act. What are we to do now?"

Georg simply looked at him, not knowing what to answer.

"Had we let them alone," Jon told him, "they might have left and never have come back."

"We don't know that. Ever since Vali Steptur fled we don't know what is going to happen!"

"Still, Georg, we don't make war with young boys, and when Tila hears of this she is going to be very angry."

"Tila is still a young girl," Georg said.

"Tila is our princess," Jon said. "Whether you like it or not, she is, for now, the titular head of the nation of Grandau and you and I are her subjects."

"Never forget, Jon, we are her advisors."

"But all decisions are hers. Never forget that, Georg . . . and I will make sure you don't."

After a moment, Georg nodded. "What do we do with them?"

"Tila will decide. If she thinks they are a threat . . . well, there is always the cliff, we cut their boat loose, and that will end it."

There was little need for the two men aboard the *Dragonfish* to fake a breakdown. Their lack of sailing skill did it for them. By the time they managed to get a line around the dock piling on Peolle, the three small boys fishing from one end were laughing so hard they almost went overboard.

Neither Aktur nor Embor liked to be laughed at, especially by kids. In their country they would have lashed out with vicious blows and those laughs would have turned to screams of pain and terror, but right now they had a job to do and couldn't afford to make enemies of anyone.

Faking a laugh, they asked the youngsters the way to the house of Vincent Damar. The boys showed them quickly enough. It was the only house on this section of the island, sitting just below the crown of the knoll.

On the way, Aktur Cilon said, "I would like to fix those kids for good. In our country they would be out working hard in the fields, not playing in the sun. They would be beaten for their attitude."

Embor nodded, agreeing with his partner. "They will be there later. We will take care of them then. We want no one alive who can recognize us anyway." He hefted the plastic suitcase he carried and pointed toward the house on the hill. "Let us hurry."

When they reached the edge of the crest they put on their prepared smiles as though they were friendly neighbors and followed the pathway to the door of Vincent Damar's home. Embor knocked, and when there was no answer, knocked again.

"There is no one here," Aktur said.

"I can see that, fool."

"Do we break in?"

Without answering, Embor tried the knob. It turned under his hand and the door swung open. "These peasants are too trusting. That is what kills them."

It only took them a minute to be sure the house was empty, and the way Embor muttered under his breath Aktur knew he was being eaten up by rage.

They had expected to find their victims at home and helpless and the pleasure of "eliminating" them would have made Embor especially happy and much easier to live with.

"What do you think?" Aktur asked.

His partner pointed to several framed pictures. They showed Vincent and Larry on the new *Blue Tuna II*, tied to the dock where the two men had left the *Dragonfish*. "That is his boat. Do you see anything familiar about it?"

Aktur looked at it closely, studying the detail. "If I'm not mistaken . . . that's the cruiser that passed us when we were coming down here."

"You're not mistaken," Embor said. "There is no doubting those lines. We are still in luck. They were going north, and between here and Miami are all known islands, not one of which would be hiding the people we look for."

"Then they'll be coming back here!"

"Probably. My guess is that they are having their boat serviced and supplied."

"Then we wait for them," Aktur said impulsively. "We can hide . . ."

"Idiot," Embor snarled, "we have no *time* to hide. We have to be the first to reach that strange island and eliminate every last one of that bunch."

"But the old man . . . the one on the tape. He is with this Vincent person."

Embor laid the plastic case on the tabletop and opened it. He took out six sticks of dynamite, their primer caps, and all the equipment to arrange a booby trap inside the house. "Here, comrade. You are the explosive expert. Put your bomb together so that it will destroy this house and everyone in it so completely there will be nothing left but dust."

A minute later Aktur had found the place. He pointed to the rocking chair beside the table. "A well-used piece of furniture, comrade. I place the charge beneath it and on the second or third rock the dynamite blows and there will be no trace of anything."

Embor was looking at a partially opened chart on the table. It was the top one of many and his eyes were going over every detail of it.

"Comrade . . . do you approve of where I put . . ."

"Yes, yes, it is fine," Embor told him impatiently. Then he began to smile. He had spotted the circle that had been drawn and retraced in an excited manner around the tiny dot of an island in the Cardiff Chain, the last speck that marked the cluster of islands. He snapped his fingers, halting his partner in his work, and waved him over. "This is where they are." He tapped the map. "A place called Montique Island."

"But . . . the old man called it Halu on the tape."

"That was *their* name for it. Now finish your job. It is time to leave."

From their place in the bushes, the three boys watched the men come down the path and search the dock area quickly. One boy said, "They are looking for us!"

"I told you they were not good men. You saw their eyes?"

"Quiet! The wind is toward them . . . they could hear us."

On the dock the men looked as if they were about to probe through all the grounds, but they seemed too much in a hurry to do something else, so with a sharp kick at an empty gas can, they got back on the *Dragonfish*, turned the engine over, flipped off their rope, and backed away from the dock.

When they were sure they were out of sight, the boys stood up. "What do you think they wanted at Mr. Damar's house?"

"They weren't there long," one of the other boys said.

The smallest boy shrugged and added, "Well, they didn't take anything. They even left something there . . . that bag they carried."

"Yeah," the other boy agreed. "They're probably Mr. Damar's friends."

"With faces like that?"

"Aw, come on. All mainlanders look like that at first." The first boy laughed.

Many thousands of miles northeast of the Caribbean, in a great fieldstone manor outside of London, England, Sir Harry Arnold was in a serious discussion with two people, one a high-ranking member of Parliament, the other an elderly man with the fine features of a scholar, but whose face for the moment bore an almost unbelieving expression. He was looking with controlled excitement at the picture Sir Harry had drawn of the ring old Vali Steptur had let them see, and his hands were trembling with passion.

"There is no doubt at all, Sir Harry. You have drawn an exact likeness of the ring seal of King Tynere! Do you know what this means?"

"From what Mr. Benson here has told me, I'm beginning to."

"When the people of my country first heard of this," he went on, "a change came over them that is hard to believe. They became a . . . a *united* country again. It was hard to suppress some of the young ones . . . they were all for throwing off the yoke of the oppressor at once."

"We still aren't certain, Mr. Milos."

"I know," Henri Milos said, "but even a rumor was enough. Now, with this . . ."

Mr. Teddy Benson, the member of Parliament from the southlands, held up his hand for attention. "Gentlemen . . . one thing we must be certain of, and that is no violence. Any outward show of force in a revolt against the neighboring country and there will be a police action that will stop any attempt at independence."

"When my people see their own chosen royal family returning," Henri Milos stated, "they will be hard to restrain. For too many years they have existed almost as slaves to their conquerors."

"Nevertheless," Mr. Benson insisted, "it will be up to the more mature men to control the situation."

Henri Milos nodded, then his eyes clouded. "There is a problem."

"What's that?"

"Our . . . enemy, as I shall call them now, knows about the existence of the Grandau royal family too. In fact, it was our informants inside their organization who brought the news to us first."

"Have they taken action yet?" Sir Harry demanded.

"Apparently so. Two of their men have been assigned to the project. They flew to Miami the same day they received the call about the tapes." He paused for a few seconds, looking at each of his friends. "These two men who were sent . . . they are bad men . . . killers. They do those terrible things their government finds necessary to stay in power."

A silence fell over the trio, then Sir Harry said, "I'll notify Vincent Damar at once." He looked at Teddy Benson and asked, "Have we any military ships in the area?"

Sadly, Teddy Benson shook his head. "Not any more. Britain no longer rules the sea."

"I'll try to radio him directly."

Benson smiled and nodded. "I'd even settle if we had the old ship of the line there now . . . the one you told me about."

"The *Tiger*," Sir Harry said. "I'm afraid there is no *Tiger* around to help those people out now."

CHAPTER 5

Right then Tila wasn't feeling like the ruling princess at all. Where before she had been insistent upon seeing the newcomers through the telescope, now she was hesitant upon viewing them in person. Her hands shook and her feet dragged as Helena and Margo led her to the low wooden building where the two boys were being held captive.

She paused at the door, hoping the older ones would call off this affair, but when she saw the expression on their faces, she knew that since she had chosen to act as a princess earlier, there was no way she could give up the role now. Whether she wanted to or not, she was their royal ruler and there was no turning back. But, princess or not, she was still only twelve years old, and having to stand face to face with a pair of those horrible outsiders, the very ones she had always been told were the enemy, was going to take every ounce of her strength.

Tila swallowed hard, took a deep breath, and stepped inside. While she still had the courage, she said as fast and as regally as she could, "I am Tila of the House of Tynere, princess of the Kingdom and of all my people and you are my prisoners!"

Larry and Josh looked at each other in puzzlement and Josh shook his head. "What did she say?"

"Beats me, but she sure is pretty."

"She looks mean, pal."

"Come on, she's only a little girl."

"Phooey," Josh grunted. "She's our age and they can get pretty mean about then."

A small grin played around Larry's mouth. "You wouldn't say that about Mary Verne, would you?"

Josh blushed and grinned back. Mary was the sister of a friend of his and lately he had been taking an interest in her since they shared the same hobbies.

It was just too much talk for Tila, however. She put her hands on her hips, stamped her foot, and turned to her friends. "*What* are they talking about? How dare they smile like that! Don't they realize that this is my kingdom and they are my prisoners?"

Helena and Margo didn't answer her. They simply smiled back and Margo said, "You'd better pay attention to your captives then, Tila. I think they're trying to tell you something."

She turned quickly, and there was Larry, holding his hand out in a gesture that even she knew. It was one of friendship, and when she looked at his face she knew he really meant it. At first she was going to ignore it, but girlish curiosity was just too much and she giggled and took his hand in hers, shook it, and reached for Josh's.

Larry realized she couldn't understand him, but he made a few motions with his hands, indicating the room, pointing to outside, and showing how he didn't know what had happened. Then he said, "It's kind of a funny way of meeting, but we're sure happy to see you." He patted his stomach and made signs of eating. "Now, if you could only find us some breakfast . . ."

"They're hungry!" Tila exclaimed.

"All boys are hungry," Helena reminded her. "But

they are your prisoners, remember?" She smiled gently, waiting.

"Well, we can still feed them, can't we?"

Testing her, Helena asked, "Suppose they escape?"

"Oh, nonsense," Tila replied. "They're only boys and we have plenty of men. Besides, where could they go? Their boat is well guarded."

"And you are not afraid of these . . . wild outsiders?"

Tila couldn't help it. She looked at Larry and Josh and giggled again. The thought of them being her captives made it seem even funnier. Here they had come from far away, sailing here themselves, totally unafraid, while she had never even been off this island.

With a forefinger, Tila tapped herself, said "Tila," then turned toward her companions and indicated, "Margo . . . Helena."

The boys understood immediately and introduced themselves. Then, like any young lady, Tila unselfconsciously reached out, took their hands, and led them out into the sunlight.

"I think our princess has found two good friends," Margo remarked.

And friends they were, right from the beginning. Everyone gathered around to meet the boys, and almost instantly they were exchanging ideas with simple sign language and identifying and naming objects about them. Larry's watch amazed them, for they told time by the sun and stars, and the tricks he did with the magnet from the toolbox astounded them. It was a day of wonderful companionship, of learning and teaching, and as the sun was beginning to set on the horizon, Larry held up his hand for everyone's attention.

When all eyes were on him, he took a stick, and

in the packed earth sketched a well-remembered design. As the men crowded in to inspect it there were sudden sharp gasps and Jon said, "That is a picture of the royal seal of Tynere!"

Georg's face was a mask of astonishment. "But where . . . could they have . . ."

Understanding came to Jon at once. *"They have found Vali Steptur!"*

Josh grinned and poked Larry's arm excitedly. "They know. Hear that . . . Vali Steptur was one of them, all right!"

It took a while for everyone to quiet down, then with sand pictures and body motions, the boys described their rescue of the old man. They realized that the group was completely unfamiliar with modern living, so couldn't give them certain details, but they made it plain that old Vali was safe and soor there would be others here at the island with all the help they needed.

That night was one they would long remember, sitting there in the brilliant moonlight, the dying embers of the fire throwing a reddish glow over everyone's face. With the excitement of youth, Tila managed to convey to the boys all of their past history, the escape from Grandau in the old leaky boat that was sinking under the party, and the rescue by a mysterious ship that came out of the fog and carried them to safety.

"The *Tiger*," Josh said softly. "The story was true after all."

Larry nodded and posed the question as best he could. He drew pictures, he acted out his thoughts, did everything he could to see if they knew whatever became of that mysterious ship that appeared so abruptly. But when they realized what he was asking, they all shook their heads and went through a pantomime of their own.

When they finished Josh said, "It was too long ago, I guess."

"Somehow," Larry told him, "I get the feeling that the ship got lost somewhere."

"But where? This isn't much of an island and from what they said, they hardly ever leave the top of it except to fish off the beach we landed on."

"That longboat came from someplace," Larry insisted.

"You drew a picture of it and nobody knew what it meant."

Larry glanced out over the shadowy faces and after a moment said, "Maybe it's a little too early to tell, Josh."

His friend wanted to know what he was getting at, but the hour was late and tomorrow was another day. Georg and Jon stood up and waved for them to follow, and with big smiles toward the assemblage and a handshake for Tila they went after the two men to the building that had been their jail earlier. This time there were comfortable beds, stools to sit on, and fresh water in a clay pitcher.

"Pretty neat," Josh observed. "Guess they sure are glad their trouble is all over."

This time it was Larry who couldn't escape a funny feeling. "Yeah," he said. "Let's hope so."

Night had closed in around the two men on board the *Dragonfish*. They had dropped anchor off a rocky little island that was one of many in the Cardiff Chain, secure in the knowledge that they were well hidden from any of the passing ships. They showed no lights and the silhouette of the *Dragonfish* blended in with the shadows of the trees on the island.

Aktur Cilon had been on the shortwave radio transmitter the past fifteen minutes, sending a detailed message as he consulted the sea charts of the area. He spoke in the native tongue of his country, but even so, the conversation was coded to keep its import from any listening ears.

When he shut down the power Embor asked brusquely, "Well?"

"Our submarine, the *Krolin*, is now five hundred miles west of our position. The captain will sail immediately for the island of Montique and wait for our signal." He paused, then added, "Now, how do you propose we proceed?"

Embor nodded thoughtfully. "It should be an easy matter. We make a landing, eliminate everyone on the island, retrieve whatever papers or information may be necessary, then leave."

"You are forgetting," Aktur frowned, "that the captain of our submarine will expect us to leave with him. How then do we make our escape?"

"Simple," Embor assured him. "We tell him we have to stay behind to be sure there has not been contact with the other island. As a matter of fact, we could deliver whoever it is of that royal family to his keeping to give him reason to get away quickly. The elimination of that one can be their problem."

"Excellent." His smile had an evil touch to it. "The best part is . . . no one even suspects that we are here, and before any can, they will all be . . . eliminated. The bomb in the house was a smart move."

Sir Harry had been on the radio for six hours straight without being able to raise Vincent Damar on Peolle Island. He knew that in his friend's different time zone they would be fast asleep with their radios shut down, but the situation was serious enough to try anything. A pair of deadly agents were aware of the information Vincent had and would be ready to do anything to keep that information from going any further. He glanced at the clock, scowled with impatience, and waited for the minute hand to make a full circle again.

Now, at Peolle Island, the sun would be coming up. He flipped the power switch of the radio to ON and picked up the microphone. At two-minute intervals he repeated Vincent Damar's call letters, then sat back and waited.

There was no answer.

A worried frown creased Sir Harry's forehead. There were killers loose and he hadn't been able to warn his friend. Desperately, he kept hoping that it wasn't too late. He picked up the microphone and tried again.

There still was no reply.

The *Blue Tuna II* was fifteen miles from Peolle when Tim came up from the galley with fresh coffee. Vincent was finishing his watch at the helm, listening to the morning news from the portable radio in the rack beside him. He took the coffee gratefully, turned the wheel over to Tim, and was about to take a break on the deck when he stopped short. He heard the news commentator mention the name "Mackley" and something made his skin crawl.

". . . apparently Mackley, the murdered man, had recently withdrawn a million dollars from his bank prior to his death. The Miami police have now definitely established the fact that the escaped convicts had nothing to do with the deceased except to discover the body minutes before they themselves were captured. At this time, there is no clue as to the whereabouts of the million dollars."

Tim gave Vincent a serious look. "Something is very bad, my friend."

"It ... may not have anything to do ... well, with Vali and that old boat."

"Do you really believe that?"

"I'm hoping," Vincent told him, "but we'd better not take any chances just the same." He switched his radio on and gave the call letters for his friend Herman up on the Florida Keys. It was ten minutes before he answered and his voice was full of sleep when he came on.

"Yeah, Herman here. What's the trouble?"

"Vince Damar, Herm. I need some information."

"When?"

"As soon as possible. Look, get on your telephone and see who you can raise at the Miami Language Institute. See if Mackley left any record of getting a letter from me."

"That dead guy?"

"Right."

"You in trouble, Vince?"

"Not so far, but if it's coming I'd like to know what we're getting into. Rush it, will you? Get somebody to open the place up if you have to."

"Where do I contact you?" Herman asked.

"On Peolle Island. We ought to be at the dock in less than an hour."

He switched off and gave Tim a concerned glance. Up ahead, Peolle was looming up in the early morning sunlight, his dock a thin finger sticking out into the deep blue waters. On the top of the hill the sun glinted off the windows of his house as though there were a fire inside. Somehow it gave him a strange feeling in his stomach.

With his usual show of good seamanship, Tim edged the *Blue Tuna II* into its berth and cut the engines while Vincent was snubbing down the bow and aft lines. When he stepped onto the dock, Tim asked, "Did you expect visitors, my friend?"

"No, why?"

"There are marks where a red rub rail has brushed the pilings. They are fresh."

"Could have been an islander."

"None we know have red rub rails. It is a superstition they have."

Vincent inspected the spots, not liking what he saw. "Possibly a transient then. They could have gone around the other side of the island when they found us gone."

"Maybe. I will see." He nodded toward the up-turned gasoline can at the corner of the dock. "They are very careless with other people's property though." He picked up the can, looked at the scuff mark made by a boot, and set it back in its place. Then, together, they started toward the house.

Halfway up the hill they could see the gentle curve of the island and the ocean licking the opposite side. Fishing boats dotted the waves, out since dawn to catch the tide and avoid the heat of day. A few figures moved on the beach, but it was still too early for the kids, busy doing their chores, to be on the eastern side.

Vincent pushed the door open and they went inside, setting their gear on the floor. Then Vincent turned his radio on, unplugged the earphones and set it for loudspeaker, and turned around to find his friend looking at the ceiling with his eyes half closed. "What's the matter, Tim?"

Tim's head turned, then it became evident what he was doing. He was smelling the air, doing something the mainlanders had never been able to accomplish. "Someone has been here, Vincent."

"You sure?"

Tim nodded, still sniffing the air. "Don't move," he said. "There is more than a foreign man-smell here."

"Can you identify it?"

"Only that it is not a good smell, my friend. There is evil in it. Something hard and evil."

Vincent didn't dispute his friend. All too well he knew how keen Tim's sense of smell was and how perceptive his island intuition. He let his eyes roam around the room, remembering the details as they were when they left. At first, things seemed untouched, but then he saw his map. He had closed it after he had used it. Now it was open to the section showing the Cardiff Chain of islands, and with a sudden touch of fear he knew he had drawn a circle around the last one in the chain, Montique Island, where the boys should be right now . . . and the remnants of a great nobility.

It was Tim that found it. His unerring sense of smell led him to the chair where Vince would have been sitting had he not stopped him in his tracks. He pointed it out and Vincent studied the booby trap until he was positive he could deactivate it, then disengaged the trigger mechanism and pulled the dynamite sticks out from under the chair. "You won't have to go looking on the other side of the island for visitors, Tim. They've been here and gone."

"Why would they do this, Vincent?"

Before he could answer, his call letters crackled from the speaker and he said, "That should be Herman or the kids."

But it was neither. Sir Harry had finally reached him and his message was brief and to the point.

Everyone's lives were in total jeopardy. The agents of that European dictatorship were vicious, deadly men.

What made it even worse was that the two Sir Harry was warning him about already had a huge lead on them and there was nobody to stop them in their deadly game except two young boys who could hardly do a thing at all.

Tim said, "The International Patrol boat is still on the rails waiting for a new propeller. It will be three days before it's in the water again."

"I know. We'll have to go ourselves. If we're lucky we'll raise the boys on the radio before they get to them. Somebody must have seen the boat that was here, so let's get a description of it and let the kids know what to look for."

With a nod, Tim headed for the door. "I hope we're not too late."

"So am I, Tim, so am I."

CHAPTER 6

The boys were up even before the sun came over the horizon. Everyone worked on the island, even visitors, and theirs was the job of bringing in the water from the natural stone cistern carved into the rock by a million rainfalls.

Ordinarily, Tila would have had little to do, but this was one day she insisted on doing her complete share, personally making breakfast for her guests. She sat between the two of them, able to say a few of their words as they did hers, but it really didn't matter at all. Somehow they got their meanings across the way all kids can.

When they finished, the treasures of Grandau were brought out and laid in front of them to inspect, and Larry whistled in admiration at what they saw.

Josh looked at him curiously. The objects were new to him. "What are they?"

"This," Larry pointed out, "is a sceptre of office. The king or queen holds it while performing official duties."

"It looks like a club."

"At one time it was, only now it's a jewel-covered symbol."

"Wonder what it's worth?"

"Millions of dollars, Josh."

"That's too rich for my blood," Josh said. "What are those other things?"

"All the trappings of royalty."

"Friend, I wouldn't want to be a king then. That sword may be pretty, but it would never cut the head off a mako shark and I sure wouldn't want to be caught out in the rain in that fancy coat."

"That's an ermine robe," Larry told him, "or rather, what's left of it. Looks like the moths had plenty of meals on the fur."

They went over all the relics that were brought out, nodding in approval as they inspected the gold and silver ornaments and when they had seen them all, Larry said to his friend, "There isn't much doubt about all this being real. I sure wish Dad were here to see this. No kidding, he'd really flip!"

At the mention of Larry's father, the boys looked at each other with stricken expressions. "We forgot to call them!" Josh gasped.

"They must be worried sick. Look, let's do it right now or they'll never let us go off on our own again."

It would be impossible to describe a radio to their new friends, so the boys simply indicated that they'd like them to go down and see their boat. When their intentions became clear, most of the people stopped smiling and a touch of fear clouded their eyes.

In his own tongue, Georg said, "Only a few have been to the waters. It is a place they are afraid of, a place where strangers might be . . ." he smiled gently, "like you." He pointed to Jon and himself. "We will go with you."

But he had forgotten about his princess. Tila pushed herself forward and stood in front of the man who towered over her, shaking her finger at him. "Shame on you, Georg, shame! You want to have all this pleasure for yourself!"

"But, princess . . . it can be dangerous . . ."

"Nonsense! Margo and Helena have both been there and if they can go so can I."

"But . . ." Georg started again.

"No 'buts,' " Tina said proudly. "I am going."

The two men looked at each other and spread their hands helplessly. She certainly *was* the princess and now she was letting them know it again. "Very well," Georg agreed, "but we take Helena and Margo with us just in case."

It wasn't quite as easy as all that, however. The rest of the group had to be assured there was absolutely no danger at all to their princess, and even then the entire population followed them to the descending path and watched every step they took until the little band was safe at the bottom.

From the excitement everyone was showing, the boys knew that their boat was what they wanted to see. The *Sea Eagle* was still anchored where they had left it, none of the guards having the nerve to try to go aboard.

Josh said, "Why don't we take them out on the inflatable raft? Tila ought to like that."

"Good idea. Watching that thing pop open ought to give them a thrill. Let's swim out and get it."

Thrill was hardly the word for it. When Larry yanked the lanyard on the CO_2 bottle and the two-man life raft came alive like a big fat sausage, the girls let out a concerted scream and Jon would have stuck his knife in it if Josh hadn't grabbed his arm.

Laughing, the boys pointed out that it was all right, pushing it into the water to show them what it was for. Then, one by one, they took them all to their boat, helped them over the side, and listened to the sounds of approval as their new friends looked over this strange marvel.

Larry went into the cabin and flipped his radio on, Jon standing right behind him, watching every move with amazement. He ran the collapsible antennae up to full height, then tuned the set to receive. He didn't have long to wait at all.

There were no call letters, no identification. It was just his father's voice, thick with fear, and he must have been yelling into the microphone. "Larry ... Josh, wherever you are, stay away from Montique. Two men ..."

A roar blotted out the next words and Jon's great fist came down on the set. The one word ... *kill* ... seemed to come through, but the next blow of the fist demolished the set completely and Jon reeled back against the cabin looking at his bleeding fist, his eyes bulging with a wild fear of the unknown.

Josh came running in, saw the wreckage, and turned to Larry. "What happened? Good golly, look at our radio!"

Larry calmed Jon down and said quietly, "It isn't his fault, Josh. I should have known better. He probably thought the radio was an enemy or something. Anyway, he reacted out of sheer terror."

By now Jon was feeling foolish about the whole thing and was glad to follow Larry's motion and go back outside again. When he was gone Josh asked, "You reach your dad?"

"Yeah."

Josh saw the expression on Larry's face and a chill went through him. "What's wrong?"

"I don't know for sure. Besides, it didn't seem to make sense. All I heard was him saying for us not to come here."

"Why would he do that?"

"Beats me, Josh. His voice sounded like he was
scared to death. He mentioned something about two
men, then Jon hit the set." He paused a moment,
frowning with his lip between his teeth, then: "I
thought he said one other word. It sounded like
kill."

"Larry . . ."

"What?"

"Your dad sure wouldn't want us to have anything to do with killing, would he?"

"Of course not."

"Then that message must have meant something
else."

Larry saw what he was getting to and nodded.
"Two men are out to kill us. That's why he wants
us away from Montique Island."

"And if they want to kill us," Josh added, "they'll
want to kill everyone else that's here."

Larry looked at the clock on the rack, then ran
topside and searched the sea in all directions. At
that moment the ocean was empty, but he knew
how fast a boat could travel, even one under sail.
Quickly, he sketched out a plan to Josh. Trying to
make a run for it at this point might expose them
to enemy action, so the best bet would be to stay on
the island where there was some help, at least.
Meanwhile, they removed the rotor from the engine's
ignition, hid it in a safe place, then stripped the
sails and put them in the rubber raft along with a
small tool kit; then they jumped in and paddled the
raft to shore, where they unloaded it. A few more
trips and all the passengers were back on the beach,
their eyes asking the question of what was happening.

It didn't take much pantomime to explain that someone who wanted to kill them was somewhere out there on that peaceful-looking ocean.

The submarine *Krolin* made contact with the *Dragonfish* forty-two miles northeast of Montique. The captain of the submarine watched with disgust at the sloppy way the trim ketch was being handled and said to his first mate, "They are clowns, they never should have been allowed out of the bathtub."

"Captain," the mate reminded him, "they have completed many very dangerous assignments."

"Bah! They do things under cover of night. They are like snakes, doing sneaky things to people who are not aware of what is happening. They may have great reputations in the dark places of our government, but that does not mean I have to like them too."

"It is our job . . ."

"Yes, yes, I know," the captain said irritably. "Unfortunately, we were the closest ship so we will assist them if necessary, but for the life of me I cannot see why a U-boat like the *Krolin* should be called for in a place like this. There can't possibly be anything more than an island war canoe to oppose us."

After two attempts, Aktur managed to get the *Dragonfish* close enough to the submarine so that a seaman could get a line aboard; then they stepped to the wet steel deck and nodded at the captain and his mate. While they were at sea, Aktur and Embor had gone over the details of their trickery until they were sure that when this affair was over they could disappear without anyone ever being the wiser. Those back home would not have firsthand knowledge, so would be easy to deceive, but the captain of the U-boat would be a wary and intelligent man and the last one to ever see them, so with him the act must be perfect.

Not really being men of the sea was a big help. They both saw the captain's scorn over their inferior boat handling and knew that as far as he was concerned, their being lost in the vastness of the ocean was something that could have been predicted.

So, for an hour, they went over the fine points of their plan to assault Montique; then when the captain gave his reluctant approval, they clambered over the side, almost falling into the ocean despite the steadying hands of the seamen, and managed, somehow, to get their engines going and pull away without crashing against the steel hull of the submarine.

"Such clods," the captain muttered, watching them slowly recede. "There must be idiots in the homeland."

"Well, sir, they managed to get here," the mate said.

"Only because the weather was clear, the sea calm, and we were able to give them a compass course to steer by. And they were lucky," he added. "They had better stay lucky if they want to stay alive. They wouldn't last long in a storm."

"Quite right, sir."

"Come, let us submerge and get to the rendezvous point. This is no place to be intercepted by any strange vessels."

Now a good mile away, Aktur Cilon and Embor Linero watched the gray cigar-shaped hull of the *Krolin* slowly sink beneath the surface until there was no sign of it at all.

"I think the good captain will now be able to write a report on the stupidity of our seamanship." Aktur laughed.

"He wouldn't be far wrong, you know," Embor replied seriously.

Disgustedly, Aktur shook his head. "Even an idiot could sail a compass course back to the Florida mainland. There are thousands of places in the islands along the way for us to hide in and we'll have all the time in the world to do it. The game is almost over, anyway. Who can stop us now?"

Aside from the jeweled ceremonial sword, there were no weapons on Montique Island. Their eating utensils and farming tools were all totally inadequate for defensive purposes and their only safety lay in being able to skillfully disguise the path to the top, and in case of an invasion, hope that a barrage of rocks might deter any enemy until help arrived.

"But aside from our dads," Josh asked, "who could come?"

Larry thought for a moment, then said, "Your dad told us no natives ever come here, right?"

Josh nodded. "There's nothing here for them, and besides, they have some silly superstition about the place."

"Well, they're not dumb, that's for sure, so if we set off a good smoky fire in the middle of this place they'll see it from the other islands and *somebody* will come looking."

There was hesitancy in Josh's voice. "I don't know. These islanders down here are pretty far away from civilization."

"It takes a man to start a fire though."

"What's wrong with lightning?"

"Nothing . . . it just doesn't make smoke signals too." Larry laughed.

"Okay, you win."

They waved Tila over and showed her what they needed and she ran to the group of men, talking excitedly. "They want a fire . . . a big one when the time comes. We'll pile up the logs and get ready to make a lot of smoke. They're sure it will attract attention."

"Nobody has ever come before."

"We've never made a lot of smoke before."

"There is a problem." Jon looked concernedly at Tila.

"Yes?"

"The lighting of it from our embers. The driftwood we will gather is so dry there is hardly any smoke. How can all this happen?"

The expression on Tila's face was so downcast that the boys had to laugh. At first she got angry and stamped her foot irritably, but Larry calmed her down and said, "All right, let's hear your problem. It can't be all that bad."

But it was to her, and with many motions imitating the billowing of smoke and showing them a piece of dry wood and a burned-out ash, she got her point across.

The boys still smiled, nodding. This time she didn't get mad a bit. Somehow she knew they had that all figured out too. When the party went down to the beach to collect the driftwood that had piled up along the shore, Larry and Josh went back to the boat, loaded a five-gallon can of gasoline and a couple quarts of oil in the life raft, and brought it back to land. When everything had been lugged to the top, Larry spilled a little of a gasoline-oil mixture on a bit of wood, then touched a match to it. The instant flame from that small stick made the group draw back in amazement, but when they saw the thick black smoke that came up from the ground, they knew the problem was ended.

Now Georg was sent to the highest part of the island with the ship's old brass spyglass. If any ship or boat came into view, the word would be passed. If it was one sailed by two men, then the island would be ready for defense.

While the boys were instructing Jon how the matches worked and where to pour the gasoline mixture when the time came, Tila walked to the edge of their encampment. Three of the men were still down below gathering the last of the wood, while behind her everyone else was busy at some assigned task.

Tila felt herself getting angry again. Here she was, their own princess, the ruler over every one of them, and she didn't have a single thing to do. Well, she thought, she could show them that she was useful as any of them and quite capable of getting about without a lot of people to help her.

She took a deep breath, stepped over the rim to the steep and dangerous path that wound its way down the side of the mountain to the beach. She got to the first cutback without slipping or sliding at all and suddenly felt very sure of herself.

Why, there's nothing to it, she thought. She didn't need anyone at all to help her! Now, wouldn't Margo and Helena be proud when she told them how she got all the way down the mountainside with no trouble whatsoever.

She was so wrapped up in her thoughts that she

didn't see the loose rock in front of her. Her foot slipped on the loose shale, twisted, and she went down in a sprawling dive, going giddily headfirst into open space. Before she could scream, she crashed against solid earth and felt her consciousness leaving her.

The *Blue Tuna II* was in trouble. Two hours ago the port engine had begun to overheat and had to be shut down before it seized up entirely. Now the starboard engine was running irregularly and losing RPMs fast. "Can you find the trouble?" Vincent yelled.

Down in the bilge, Tim shook his head. "I found the break in the lines, but this is the best I can do. We won't get any more power from this engine until we get back to Peolle or find some spare parts."

"We're running out of time!"

Tim finished the repairs, wiped the grease off his arms, and went topside. "How about the International Patrol?"

"They're sending the old boat out of Miami, but you know how slow *that* tub is."

"And still nothing from the boys?"

Vincent wiped his hands across his eyes. "Not a thing. All I can hope for is that they picked up one of our transmissions."

"Maybe Sir Harry could do something through his government."

"Tim . . . you don't deal with governments anymore. You deal with bureaucracies that check everything out before they move at all. If any government acted hastily it could blow up into an international incident, and *that* nobody wants."

"Things do not look good, do they? Even our

engines are against us. But we can always run the port engine for fifteen-minute periods, my friend. It takes that long to get to overheating."

"Okay," Vincent said, "let's push them to the limit. We can't let time run out on us."

Embor Linero took the binoculars out of the case and raised them to his eyes to scan the horizon. According to his calculations, Montique Island should be dead ahead. He focused slowly, then he saw what he was looking for. He climbed down from the top of the cabin and stood beside Aktur. "Give us full speed, comrade."

Reluctantly, Aktur pushed the throttle forward. "Do you really think we should charge in like this?"

Embor shrugged. "Why not? We know we eliminated the others back on the island so there would be no alert, and besides, surprise would only be in our favor."

"I don't mean that," Aktur said. He indicated the fuel gauge. "We are low on gasoline."

"We do not know enough about sails to try and maneuver in close. We will use our engine until this is over, and then, very leisurely, we can sail off to our pleasures, learning how to work that silly canvas as we go."

An hour later the *Dragonfish* lay a quarter mile off the rocky mountain that was Montique Island. From his position in the bow, Embor surveyed the rugged terrain, then picked up the *Sea Eagle* anchored off the tiny beach. "Ah, yes," he said, "they are all there, waiting like a nest of ants to be eliminated."

"But where?" Aktur asked. "I can see no one at all!"

Embor raised the glasses until the rim of the mountaintop came into view. "Where else could they be, Aktur?" Suddenly he caught the barest glimpse of something moving in the rocks. "They are up there, of course." He put the glasses back in his case and stowed them away in the rack. From the overhead he took down a rifle, checking the ammunition in the clip, and put it back on its hooks.

"Drop the anchor," he said. "The time has come."

CHAPTER 7

They had been watching the progress of the *Dragonfish* since it first appeared on the horizon, then Larry took over the spyglass and extended it to full power. He let Josh look at the boat and the two aboard and asked, "What do you think, Josh?"

"I have seen many tourists in these waters, but not quite like these. Their faces are not like . . . well, Americanos. Their clothes are not right, either."

Larry took the glass back and peered through it. "Notice the way they've dropped the sails?"

"Yes . . . like someone who never saw a sail before. They're running under power."

He could see the one called Embor scanning the island through his glasses too, saw him put them up and take down the gun from its rack. A minute later the anchor went over the side.

Jon tapped him on the shoulder and pointed toward the piled logs in the background. Larry shook his head. The sun was sinking below the horizon now, and before they could get the smoke up it would be too dark to see it. All that would be visible would be light from the fire, and on the mountaintop in the dark of night, that might only add to native superstition and keep them further away than ever.

"Everything ready, Josh?"

"The men are in their places," he answered.

"The trail covered up?"

"If they find it at all, it will take plenty of time. And if they do, they'll still have to climb it. We have enough throwing stones to drive them back."

"Josh . . . they have guns, and these people have never seen what one can do."

For a moment Josh had a faraway look on his face. "It's almost like it was before, when they had to run from the same enemy in Grandau."

"Yeah, only this time there's no *Tiger* coming in under full sail to rescue them."

"Who knows, Larry? We did see its longboat."

Larry shot him a curious look. "Remember," he finally said, "how no one recognized the sketch we made of the longboat . . . or the letters of its name we drew in the sand?"

"Yes. It was very odd."

"Yet the longboat was very real and Vali Steptur knew where it was."

"Then why wouldn't he have used it sooner, or at least told someone else about it?"

"I'm guessing on this," Larry told him, "but I think he put more faith in the old story than the others did. To them it was a legend . . . to him something real. He was getting old and knew they'd laugh at him, so he set out to locate it and he did."

"But this island is barely a mile across!"

"You can lose track of a lot of things in a mile," Larry said.

Overhead the last of the fading light went into the darkness of night. From the west came the low rumble of thunder, and the faint glow of sheet lightning made billowing clouds glow yellow momentarily. There was a coolness in the air now, along with the smell of rain.

For those standing guard along the rim, woven

palm-leaf poncholike hoods were handed out. Larry and Josh took theirs from Margo and thanked her. She still had one left in her arms and asked, "Tila?"

The boys looked at each other and shook their heads. They hadn't seen Tila since they'd taken up their posts and assumed she was safe in one of the houses. Margo gave them an anxious nod and went off, calling for her princess.

Once again, Larry aimed the spyglass at the beach and peered through the eyepiece.

"See anything?"

"Nothing." He collapsed the glass down into the big section and folded the brass cap over the lens. "This antique was made for daylight only. Now I appreciate the refinements of modern night glasses."

"Too bad we didn't think to bring ours."

"Well," Larry said, "it's too late now."

They were interrupted again as the first drops of rain reached them. Margo's face was frightened, her voice hoarse when she asked, "Tila . . . Tila?" then went off into a flurry of her own language. Right behind her Georg came up and waited for their answer. When the boys shook their heads the frozen look that crossed Georg's eyes told them everything.

Tila had disappeared from the island.

It was the rain that awakened her. It was slashing with windswept fury across her face and a cold shudder racked her body. She moaned softly and opened her eyes, wondering where she was and why somebody wasn't taking care of her the way they always had.

A jagged streak of lightning split the night apart and for a brief second she saw where she was, caught in the rocks halfway down the side of the mountain, and she knew she was there because she didn't want anyone taking care of her. Tears welled into her eyes, but she fought them back and tried to get her foot out of the crevice of rock that trapped her.

She had to give up. Her strength was giving out and her foot was still wedged in too tightly for her to get loose alone. For a while she lay there, breathing deeply, the cool rain making her alert again, then she began to yell for help as loud as she could. Twice there was a flash of lightning and the almost immediate burst of thunder drowned her out, then she yelled again. She knew her voice was getting hoarser every time she cried out, yet she dared not stop. All too often she had seen these heavy rains cut into the weathered sides of the mountain and break loose the flat shale that tore even bigger chunks out of the rock until there was another avalanche of sharp, deadly rubble sweeping down the steepness and piling into the ocean at the base with a roar that got lost in the spray it generated.

Tila pushed herself partially erect, looking toward the top of her mountain. There was nothing but blackness there and the rain tore at her face. She felt the first bite of stone particles hit her too and knew some of the aged facing stone was beginning to loosen.

Once more, she thought. I can yell for help just once more. If there is no answer, then I will go down the rockslide and the House of Tynere will have come to an end.

She took a deep breath and screamed as hard as she could.

The voice that answered said, "Well, well, what have we here?"

*But it wasn't in her language or the one the boys
used either, and the tone of it was hard and flat.*

Then, when the lightning came again, she saw
the faces of the two men, recognized the deadly
menace in their expressions, and knew then who
they were and once more she screamed until there
was no voice left in her at all.

High up above, Josh stiffened and turned his head
ever so slightly. The strange ways of the storm had
made the wind twist back on itself, and his ears, so
finely tuned to nature, had caught something that
should not have been there.

"What is it, Josh?" Larry had seen his friend
being suddenly alerted.

"It sounded like . . . a scream."

"You sure?"

He listened intently, every nerve on edge, ready
to catch even the faintest note of that same sound.
But there was none. He looked at Larry a few
seconds, then nodded. "I'm sure. It was a scream,
all right."

Softly, Larry asked, "An animal, perhaps?"

"No. It was a person."

And they both were thinking the same thing. The
only person missing was Tila.

Larry knew how perceptive his friend's trained
senses were and he was almost afraid to ask, but he
had to. "Could you identify the voice?"

Josh confirmed his fears. "It was a girl's."

In back of them the search was still going on
in the area and they knew there wasn't time to
get help. Tila was someplace down the mountain,
stranded in the storm and possibly hurt, and what
counted right then was speed. Only Margo, who
was still looking for Tila around the rim, saw them

motion to her that they were going down the side, but she didn't have the faintest idea why because she was certain Tila never would have gone down there anyway.

Two minutes after they had stepped onto the sheer slippery wet path the boys knew they had trouble. The rain had turned their footing into a mucky, slippery chute that could whip their feet out from under them and send them crashing to their death. Luckily, the roots of the bushes that lined the path were still holding fast, so that when they slipped they were able to regain their footing. At one turn Larry went down, his fingers barely hanging onto the stub of a dead bush until Josh gave him a hand, and before he could stand up his canvas shoes kicked loose a ridge of shale and sent it bouncing down into the darkness.

That same shale sprayed itself over Embor and Aktur as they yanked at Tila's arms. She beat at them, but they held her wrists until she stopped and Aktur said, "Why not leave her be? She won't last long here in this storm. Who could she tell about us then?"

Embor agreed and gave her arms another wrench. "She's only a stupid girl anyway."

The pain in her arms brought life back to Tila. In her most commanding voice she shouted at them hoarsely, "How dare you touch me like that, you beasts! Take your hands off me. I am the Princess Tila of the House of Tynere, the ruler of the Kingdom of Grandau. For this insult . . ."

Aktur raised his hand to slap her, but Embor stopped him short.

"What is it?" Aktur asked impatiently. "We can't afford to waste time and . . ."

"Silence, you clod. It's too bad you don't use your

ears for listening to other people." He grinned and
twisted those small arms again and heard her voice
lash out at him again. He looked up at Aktur and
said, "Did you hear it then, comrade?"

A frown of puzzlement was on Aktur's face. "I
heard *Tynere* and *Grandau*, but . . ."

"It's such a pity you didn't go further in the study
of languages," Embor told him. "She said something
else . . . *princess* . . . and *Tila*. What we have right
here, comrade, is the precious jewel in this whole
search of ours. She is the last of the royal line of
Tynere and when we deliver her to our people, who
will get the story from her before her . . . er . . .
elimination, our job is done."

"There are those up there that must be taken
care of too," Aktur said.

"Certainly." Embor grinned evilly. "But why
should we risk our necks on this mountain when
our submarine can simply fire in high-explosive
shells from its deck gun. I am certain the good
captain would be happy to have a piece of the action
knowing a medal and promotion would await him
in the motherland."

The other man returned the evil grin and nodded.
"Embor, you are right. Let us get her out of these
rocks and back to our boat. I can almost taste those
wonderful things our money is going to buy us in
the United States."

"First we must get there."

"Of course." Aktur laughed. "And what could be
easier?"

It was the glaring brightness of the lightning
that made them see it. Right in front of their faces,
snagged on the broken end of a twisted, half-uprooted
bush was a piece of old fabric. The swirling gusts

had almost ripped it away when Larry grabbed it. They both looked at it and knew what it was. The last time they had seen it, it was part of a dress Tila wore.

They waited for another sharp flash of lightning, and this time they knew what to look for. They saw the path of broken bushes that had partially cushioned the falling body of their new friend. Without waiting, they stepped off the time-traveled narrow road down and slipped and fought a muddy battle following the trail of bent foliage and a few more pieces of fabric until they slid into a rock pile gasping for breath.

"She's got . . . to be here," Josh gasped. "There are . . . no more bushes. All rocks now."

"Suppose she isn't?"

"Then . . . she went into the ocean. It's all over."

They had to wait for another flash from the night sky before they could be sure and they looked up, worried. The storm was drifting past quickly and the rain was beginning to diminish. Then it came, and they were able to look into the cluster of rocks beside them.

Another piece of fabric was caught on a shale outcropping, but there was no young girl there at all. The total shock of it broke over the boys like an icy wave and they could taste the bitter disappointment in their mouths. "We're too late," Larry barely whispered.

Josh would have agreed with him, but the final flash of lightning showed him something so startling he scarcely believed it. In that tiny moment of time when everything was daylight, bright with intense electrical energy, he had seen the imprint of booted feet in the wet earth and they were leading downward toward the beach!

There was no time for disappointment now. At least Tila was still alive. If she weren't they would have left her there. It was evident now what the two men had planned. They were going to stage their attack at night with the storm as cover, but they had heard Tila scream and had gone to investigate. Knowing how she would have reacted to her capture, the boys were sure it wouldn't take those men long to realize what a prize they had taken!

"How long has it been since we started?"

Larry checked his watch. "Forty-five minutes."

"They have a good start."

"She won't make it easy for them to carry her. We could still catch up."

"Then what, Larry? How do we get past their guns?"

"I don't know. We're just going to have to find out."

With the strange suddenness so typical in tropical lands, the storm above broke and the rolling clouds drifted by to let the soft glow of moonlight spill down. In a few minutes their eyes adjusted to it and they were able to position themselves. To one side the old path cut by and they'd be able to follow it down to the shoreline.

Pointing downward, Josh said, "Look."

The men's forms were indistinct, but they were visible, two blobs struggling with something between them. They could hear guttural sounds now and occasionally Tila's biting voice until it was sharply cut off.

As quickly as they could, the boys scrambled downward, the rushing water still coursing down the mountainside covering any noise they made. When they reached the sand, breathing heavily from their exertion, they saw what had happened.

Tila *had* been a heavy bundle for them. She must have been kicking and twisting every minute of the time and now they had tied her up and tossed her on the sand while they sprawled out to get their wind back. They were only a few feet from the water and the dinghy from their boat was at the now quiet surf's edge ready for launching. Plainly, they could see the rifles the men held and the holstered pistols on their belts.

Neither boy wasted time discussing the impossibility of the situation. Their own life raft was too far away and too well hidden to go for at this point and they both realized it. "There is one thing we can do, Josh."

"You name it, friend."

"I'm going to swim out to their boat. If I can get there ahead of them maybe I can disable it."

Josh's mouth dropped open. "In *these* waters at night? There are sharks out there and this is their feeding time!"

"You have a better idea?"

Slowly, Josh shook his head.

"Then I'm going," Larry told him. "What you do is run interference for me. When those men get ready to move, get in the shadows and throw rocks or shells or anything at them. Keep moving around so they'll think there's more than just one person, but keep them stirred up so I can get a jump on them."

Josh's concern was intense. "Look, you're risking your life when . . ."

But Larry cut him off. "Buddy, this isn't the islands. These are city people and I know how the city people are. You don't think they're going to let her live, do you?"

"They can't just kill her!"

"Why not? Power and money is more important to their kind than life. No, if they get away with her, she is dead. Now go ahead and keep your eyes on those two."

Before Josh could stop him, Larry was wading silently into the water. He scarcely made a ripple, and Josh turned and went back into the darkness of the shadow of the mountain. Above him the moon was a huge white face beaming down and at any other time it would have been a beautiful sight. Now it was a danger. He searched around, gathered some good-sized rocks, and picked out his first position.

In the water, Larry breaststroked slowly. He was well aware of the fact that sharks were there and *did* feed at night, and he knew any noise or vibration that resembled that of an injured or dying fish would attract them long before his scent reached them. Inwardly, he wanted to flail away at the sea with a racing stroke to get there as fast as possible, and it took all of his concentration not to.

He passed the point where the *Sea Eagle* was still riding at anchor, wondering what else the two men had done to disable it. A few hundred yards ahead, in the glow of the moonlight, he could see the men's ketch where it was moored in deeper water. He could feel his heart thudding now, because this was the critical time, swimming in the area where the sharks could be cruising. Behind him he heard a sudden yell in a strange language, then another and another, and he knew that Josh was creating a diversion. He began swimming again, still quietly, but with stronger arm movements.

Something caught his eye to one side. Was it real, or did he imagine he had spotted the outline of a triangular fin cutting a swath through the water?

He looked again, but there was nothing there. He could feel the panic creeping up on him because he knew the first attack, if it came, would probably be from beneath. He forced himself to stop and take several deep breaths to calm himself down; then he looked back toward the beach. There was something else back there and he knew what it was.

The men had gotten their dinghy into the water.

He couldn't waste another second. He had to take the chance now or risk losing the whole game. Sharks or no sharks, he broke into a speed stroke, arms digging into the water, feet beating in tempo as he churned his way to the boat ahead.

The moon threw a broad swath of rippled light across the water and he saw the fin cross it and disappear. It came back again, the direction reversed and nearer this time. Fear gave Larry a new burst of energy, and he put everything he had into the last few strokes that took him to the side of the *Dragonfish*.

And right behind him now was a fin angling toward him.

The men had left the ladder over the side for their return and Larry grabbed the rungs and hauled himself out of the water just as that huge gray body slid by beneath him. When he rolled onto the deck he had to lie there a few seconds just to get his breath back. They were a few seconds he could scarcely afford.

Ten yards away one man was pulling hard on the dinghy's oars while the other was tightly holding an enraged young girl to keep her from struggling. Larry only allowed himself that one look, then he crawled to the cabin, staying low and out of sight. He fumbled for the hatch cover over the engine, ran his hands around the edges feeling for the latch, but there was none, and he realized it was a remote-opening lock ... he wasn't going to be able to disable the engine after all.

One thing he did see ... and that was the key in the ignition lock. He yanked it out, dropping it into his pocket as the dinghy bumped the hull of the boat. He heard the key clink against the magnet in his pocket and grinned. There still was something he could do. He fingered the small magnet loose, stuck it behind the boom. Canvas was flopping loosely all over the place, and whenever he felt a rope he slashed his knife through it. He saw the men come over the side, pulling Tila with them. There was little he could do now, but as for those men, even if they could manage to hot-wire the engine and get it started, they'd follow a wild course with the magnet scrambling their compass, and there was no way at all they were going to be able to raise any canvas without a major repair job.

Larry watched while the men dragged the girl forward and tied her down. Next to him he could hear the gentle rub of the dinghy against the ketch, and while the others' heads were turned he dropped over the side silently, got into the dinghy, detached the line, and shoved it away from the boat. He was well in the dark when he heard the muffled voices of the men. Then there was silence a moment, the cabin door slammed, and a muted nasty remark was passed before the engine turned over, caught, then idled while the men pulled up the anchor.

Someplace, they had had a spare key.

Now it was all up to that little piece of magnetic metal, Larry thought.

CHAPTER 8

"What will be our heading, Embor?"

"Eighty degrees at twelve hundred RPMs for one hour ten minutes. That will put us within range of the *Krolin*'s radar and they can contact us."

Aktur Cilon turned the wheel and let the compass settle on the slightly northeast heading. He looked up, but there was cloud cover over the moon again and another rumble of thunder in the west.

Dratted tropical weather, he thought. There was no way you could rely upon it to remain stable. Now there were no stars visible, no moon to go by, and he had a very peculiar feeling about the direction they were taking. Finally he said, "Embor, are you certain we are headed properly?"

"What is your compass course?" Embor replied tartly.

"Exactly eighty degrees."

"In that case, you idiot, you are going correctly. Now pay attention to your steering while I attend to the girl."

"What will they think when they find the dinghy gone, Larry?"

"Nothing, most likely. I left the rope dangling from their rail so they'll figure it just came loose."

The two boys were standing on the deck of the

Sea Eagle, Larry looking eastward through their night glasses. "Still see them?"

"Barely," Larry answered. "They seem to be swinging in a wide circle to the south."

"But ... that's empty ocean for five hundred miles."

"They don't know that. Right now they're following a compass course."

"Wouldn't that magnet keep it steady?"

Larry lowered the glasses and shook his head. "It's probably sliding around with the motion of the boat. I never figured on that." He peered through the eyepieces again. The dim spot of light from the cabin of the *Dragonfish* was still visible. It stayed within the scope of the glasses another few minutes then was blanked out. The edge of the cliffs of Montique Island had cut them off.

Now they had to play a waiting game. Somewhere out there would be their father, but he too was strangely late. If it got there in time the *Blue Tuna II* would certainly be more than a match for the *Dragonfish,* but the time they had left had reached zero. Tila was gone, the men were out of sight, and the boys were alone.

More to keep their spirits up than anything else, they lowered the rest of their supplies, including all the spare gasoline, medicines, and foodstuffs, into the dinghy and rowed it ashore to be hidden with the other load. They wanted to leave nothing of any value to the enemy if they came back again.

By Larry's watch it was almost midnight, but there was no thought of sleeping yet. Josh had come back from his scouting trip and led Larry to the edge of the water. The tide had receded a good ten feet from the rocks and he said, "There's a natural sand strip all the way around at low tide.

Once we're on the other side there has to be some
way we can get up on the cliff and keep that ketch
in sight."

"That's good enough. Let's try it," Larry said.

They went single file with Josh in the lead, his
feet feeling out all the sure places and staying clear
of the soft, water-filled traps that could suck them
under. They wound in and out of the irregularities
in the face of the cliff, realizing they were in an
area never explored by the inhabitants of the top of
the mountain island. Twice Josh spotted the dot of
light at sea and Larry picked it up in his glasses. It
was the *Dragonfish*, all right, and the second time
it seemed to be closer.

They were both so engrossed with trying to keep
the ketch in sight that they didn't notice the strange
sound that seemed to come to them through the
rocks themselves. When they finally sensed it they
came to a stop, listening intently. The sound had a
surging quality and there was an odd smell in the
air, different from the salty tang of the ocean.

Larry said, "That sounds like wave action."

"But the ocean has quieted. There is hardly any
surf at all."

"I know ... but do you hear how muffled it is,
yet how it seems to beat like a giant drum?"

Josh's eyes narrowed and his head tilted back. It
was a common gesture and Larry knew he was
smelling the air again. "That's a freshwater smell,
friend."

"Here ... on the edge of the ocean?" Larry
queried.

"There's a cave nearby," Josh said simply.

"What!"

"A big cave, Larry, and it is acting like a drum,
making the sound of the water bigger as it runs out

with the tide." He paused, listening again. "It is someplace ahead . . . the way we must go anyway."

Carefully, they made their way around a projecting spur of rock just as the cloud cover thinned out and let the full moon throw a feeble glow around them. Josh stopped suddenly, his finger pointing. "There's their boat!"

The *Dragonfish* had changed course again, veering a good twenty degrees to the east. It was evident that the magnet Larry had left behind the compass had thrown the men into following an erratic heading, but now it could lead the ketch out of sight.

"We're going to have to get up the cliff face, Josh."

"I know. We'll follow this shoreline a little longer and if there is any kind of cave ahead, there might be a way we can climb around it."

Once again the cloud pattern broke and let the moonlight through. For the moment the sand, the sea, and the side of Montique were visible in muted detail and they took advantage of it and worked their way ahead as quickly as possible. The sandy area had widened as the tide reached its peak ebb, and the dull roaring was louder with every step they took.

When they cut around the angular column of rock that swept like a crescent from the mountain, they stopped in sheer amazement and saw something so incredible that the hair stood up on the back of their necks and made their flesh crawl all over.

It was a huge stone mouth in the solid rock, with deep black water running out of it like a living tongue and a voice of thunder coming from the depths of its throat. The overhanging brow of the cliff kept it from being seen from above and the sheltering cheek of the great crescent and its natural camouflaging color made it invisible from the sea.

The wild mystery of this phenomenon drew them closer. There was no way they could resist standing in front of that gigantic cavern, and when they felt the winds trying to suck them into the opening they realized what caused the booming sounds like invisible waves.

On either side of the wide stream that passed back and forth from the ocean to the cave were the white sands of the beach that reflected the moonlight into the monstrous hole. When they had taken only two steps inside they were frozen in their tracks by the huge form that looked like a great bat about to sweep down and devour them alive.

Both the boys were gripping each other so hard they let out grunts of pain, and Josh said, "What . . . what is it?"

Larry knew what it was, all right. It was absolutely unbelievable, but there it was, and absolutely real. It was there where the vagaries of the wind and tide had selected to put it and nature had chosen to preserve it. It was there, wet and slimy, with wings spread over the black fighting body that had iron teeth projecting from each side.

"It's the *Tiger*," Larry said.

"What?"

"Now we know what happened to it, Josh. She followed the push of the winds and the pull of the currents across the ocean until she was sucked into this cave, where she could go no further."

"But . . ."

"You smelled it earlier," Larry reminded him. He reached down, dipped his hand in the water, and tasted it. "Fresh water, Josh. Someplace there must be a mighty spring of fresh water feeding itself into this basin."

"Larry . . . even fresh water can rot wood."

"Not always."

"Back on Peolle . . ."

"That's surface water there, Josh. Apparently this water has a mineral content that preserves wood and metal long past normal expectations."

"Look at those sails," Josh insisted. "They still wave in the wind. You'd think they'd be the first to go."

"That same chemical preservative must be part of the atmosphere here. There isn't any other explanation."

Without being aware of what they were doing, they had walked around the edge of the tremendous underground pool, staying on the rock shelf that acted as a natural pier. Beyond where they were the darkness was too dense and they dared go no further.

"Vali Steptur must have found this place too," Josh said.

"There probably were old stories and legends that he remembered. At least he believed them enough to try to prove that they were true."

"Larry . . . do you think . . . we ought to go aboard?"

"Do you remember what Sir Harry told us about the *Tiger* . . . how they fitted her out for a complete cruise before they turned her loose?"

Josh nodded, wondering what his friend was getting at.

"That means the *Tiger* would have full stores of powder and cannonballs aboard. *Black powder*," he emphasized.

Josh wasn't very familiar with explosives and

said, "But black powder isn't nearly as strong as the modern stuff."

"Right," Larry agreed, "but the longer it sits, the more unstable it gets. After a long while, even the slightest disturbance could set it off, and with all the barrels of it on this ship, if that happened this island would be blown to smithereens."

"Good golly! And those people have been living with this beneath them all these years." He thought of something else and said, "What about the hurricanes and the earthquake they had here?"

"Back then the powder wasn't as unstable as it is now."

"Maybe we ought to get out of here," Josh suggested uneasily.

"I know," Larry replied. "There's something even more important than the *Tiger*."

"Tila."

Without another word they started picking their way back to the opening of the cave. Outside, the faintest gray lay on the eastern horizon. It was what was known as false dawn, the early light that goes ahead of the sunrise.

But that wasn't what worried the boys. The tide was coming back in and had already closed off the pathway in their original direction. The only thing they could do now was go back, and go back quickly. Had it been darker, they both would have certainly been caught in the treacherous sand traps or had their feet washed out from under them. But fear gave them wings and made them step carefully, hands scrabbling for holds in the rock, their breath whistling through parched throats.

It seemed as if hours had passed, but they made the final turn around the bleak stone and collapsed on the edge of the beach just as the sun began its ascent over the ocean, bathing the world in an eerie early red light.

And that strange morning glow illuminated a sight that filled the boys with a new source of strength because out there, wedged on the rocks where the falling sea had stranded it, was the *Dragonfish*!

From behind the protection of mussel-covered rocks, the boys scanned the ketch through the binoculars. It was perched there like a model ship on its stand, but apparently it was undamaged and the two men in the cabin were waiting for the tide to rise and float it off. Up on the forward deck, still tied down, was Tila. She wasn't yelling or squirming now. She was motionless, her face pale white and haggard-looking. For a moment Larry thought she was dead, but her head turned slightly and he knew she was only unconscious.

The two men came out of the cabin and peered over the listing port side, and again their voices could be heard in heated argument. Larry asked, "Think they can get her off?"

Josh nodded toward the watermarks on the side of the cliff. "There's a five-foot tide here. If she didn't get jammed in with too much force, they could make it."

"How long before the tide's in far enough?"

"Two hours."

"We have that long to get Tila back then."

"Maybe we should get some help," Josh suggested.

"No way. They'd spot us on the sand and pick us off with their rifles. Besides, we could never get up that cliff and back in time."

"What do we do then?"

Larry looked through the glasses again. "We're

going to outthink those guys on the boat, that's what."

"Oh, great. How are we going to know what *they're* thinking?"

With a little grin twisting his mouth, Larry said, "We know what they're going to *have* to think. Right now what's in their minds is getting that boat free. They can't trust the sea to come in high enough, so they're going to have to help it when it does. So . . ."

"So they lighten the load and get ready to haul it off," Josh finished for him.

"You got it," Larry said.

"I have an idiot for a partner," Embor said harshly. He studied the rocks surrounding the *Dragonfish* and grimaced in disgust. "How could you have steered right back from where you started?"

"I tell you, I followed your instructions. The compass course you gave me . . ."

"Bah! Then why are we here?"

"Didn't you check the compass three times yourself?" Aktur demanded. "Was I not right on eighty degrees?"

Sourly, Embor said, "True, but what course were you on when I was *not* looking?"

"I'm telling you . . ."

"Forget it, Aktur. It is too late for excuses. What we must do is get this boat afloat. Then, with our naked eyes and without you following a compass course, we will get away from this accursed place. Let us hope the submarine is still waiting for us."

Aktur Cilon was too tired to bother arguing back. He simply asked, "What is your plan?"

"The book describes an activity called kedging. We carry the anchor out, sink it in the bottom, then pulling on the line together, we can haul this boat off."

"It is too bad the dinghy broke loose. We could have carried the anchor in that."

"Stupid," Embor hissed. "It didn't *break* loose. You didn't tie it tightly enough. Now go up there and get the girl off the deck and put her in the stern. Because of your stupidity we'll have to walk that anchor out there while the tide is still below our heads."

There are times when thinking and waiting must stop and action come into play, even when the odds against success are ten to one. The boys knew that this was their last chance to get to Tila, a slim, final chance that could well wind up with all of them facing a bleak end.

Out there the men were doing exactly as Larry and Josh thought they would, even to removing Tila from the forward deck to make room to lay out the anchor and as much rope as they had in the locker below. The men stripped down to their shorts. Then with much arguing they went over the side, dragging the anchor with them. They distributed the weight between them, then started to plod forward. From what Larry could see, there was at least three hundred feet of line on the deck and the men would probably use at least half of it.

He tapped Josh on the shoulder and said, "Let's go."

Together, they lowered themselves into the water, not daring to wade at all. With matching breaststrokes they went directly toward the ketch, keeping the hull between them and the men's line of vision. There was no holding back now and every stroke was strong and sure, taking them right under the stern of the boat.

Propping themselves on the rocks, they hoisted themselves aboard and slithered toward the bound figure of Tila. Josh grabbed her and pulled her toward the transom, then unbound her hands and started to take the gag out of her mouth. For a second her eyes opened and she started to scream, then Josh's hand closed over her mouth until she recognized him and became still. He lowered her to Larry, went in after her, and the two of them swam back with Tila floating face up, their arms under hers and their hands locked behind her back.

When they reached the shore they stumbled up the sand to the relative safety of the low brush and trees and kept going to get as far away from the *Dragonfish* as possible. They stopped when they were out of breath and eased themselves, gasping, down onto the cool earth. And as tired as she was, Tila gave them both the warmest smile of gratitude they had ever seen and reached for their hands.

Right then Larry and Josh knew that they weren't just two friends anymore . . . they were *three*.

And as they all acknowledged the new friendship with big grins, they heard the bullets whine overhead and smack into the trees, with the delayed slam of the rifle shot a moment later.

Fury had turned Embor Linero's face a mottled red and he fired round after round into the foliage on the shore. He looked at his partner, who stood there with a rifle hanging from his arms, and yelled, "Shoot, you fool, shoot!"

"But I see no one!"

"Where else can they be? They are hiding in the brush. Cover the area now!"

Not wanting to arouse Embor's anger any further, Aktur raised the rifle and fired aimlessly into the trees, spacing his shots about ten feet apart. He kept one eye discreetly on Embor, knowing his temper. Ever since they had come back on board to find the girl gone and signs of those who had freed her on the transom, Embor had been like a madman. They couldn't leave the *Dragonfish* now lest it float free and follow the offshore breeze out to the end of the anchor line in the deeper water where the sharks were. If only Embor hadn't been in such a hurry . . .

"There . . . shoot there!" Embor hollered. He fired a single shot to mark the place where he saw the motion in the treeline, and then both men opened up with rapid fire, reloaded, and fired another magazine into the area. Embor grabbed his binoculars and focused them on the beach. At first he saw nothing and hope was beginning to rise that the intense firepower had gotten all of them, then he saw another flash of movement and muttered under his breath and put his rifle back to his shoulder. Aktur watched where the shots were hitting, then sprayed bullets on one end of the section.

A falling branch loosened by the second burst of gunfire had cut Tila's shoulder, and sand from a whining ricochet stung the boy's bodies. They knew the men had pinpointed their position when they made their last move toward new cover, and only the small sand mound they crouched behind kept them from being killed . . . and even now bullets were eating into their scanty protection.

"We can't stay here much longer, Larry."

"I know. We can't stay grouped together in one

target either. Somehow, we have to break up their fire."

"We have to get *rid* of it, Larry."

A couple of hundred yards away the *Dragonfish* had righted herself on the incoming tide and the men had a level platform to shoot from. "They could haul her off now if they wanted to," Josh said.

"What for? We have their prize and they have us pinned down."

"Somehow we've got to get them out of here."

Larry started grinning again. "You've got it, Josh, and I think I have the answer."

"Fine, just fine," Josh grunted. "I can see kids like us running off two grown men with high-powered guns and plenty of ammunition." He paused, then started grinning himself. "How do you figure to do it?"

"Think you can manage to get back down the beach a ways and draw their fire while you stay covered?"

"Sure."

"Good. Get to it then while I make Tila understand she's to stay right here with her head down."

"And what are you going to do?" Josh asked.

"Use a little firepower of our own," Larry told him.

They had to wait another five minutes before there was a lull in the shooting, then Larry nodded and said, "Go!" and all three went into action. While Tila burrowed into the sand, the boys went from tree to tree in opposite directions, and when the gunfire started again it was separated, no longer after a single grouped target.

Every tree became his fortress and Larry darted from one to another. Fifty feet more and he could lose himself in the thick undergrowth, and from there to the hidden cache of supplies would only take a few minutes. It seemed an eternity, but he finally made it and pulled himself to the spot he wanted. Right in front of him were the spare five-gallon cans of gasoline.

Luckily, the wind was right and his cover was excellent. The gentle morning breeze didn't leave a ripple on the water's surface, and when he unscrewed the cap and tipped the can, the gasoline burbled out to float in a multicolored slick away from the shore directly toward the *Dragonfish,* already bobbing gently in the rising tide. The last two cans of gasoline were added to the first, then it was done. Larry ripped open the waterproofed packet of matches from the supplies, lit one, and tossed it out on the volatile slick. Almost instantaneously, the whole ocean seemed to erupt in flame.

On board the *Dragonfish,* Embor Linero and Aktur Cilon saw the smoking destruction being blown toward them and dropped their rifles. Gone was the idea of reclaiming their former captive. Right now they had to save their own necks. With one accord they ran to the prow, grabbed the anchor line, and screamed at each other to pull, pull! They leaned into the taut rope with fear giving them strength, and just before the flames got to them the *Dragonfish* floated free, with the keel rasping against the rocks. The two men cut the line, got into the cabin, and started the engine.

Montique Island and its inhabitants had been too much for them. Now the submarine *Krolin* could stand off and blast that chunk of rock and its people to bits with its deck gun.

The boys were too hurried to cheer their victory. They grabbed Tila and got to the path that led to the top. They were bedraggled and tired and suddenly every step was an effort. That plateau on top was a long way off, an almost impossible climb in their condition, and they wondered how they were ever going to make it.

But then they heard the faint shouts and saw the men snaking their way down the path to meet them, and they knew they were safe. At least for now. Help was on its way and the fire barrier kept the *Dragonfish* off. Most of the flame was gone now, but the men were taking no chances any longer. The ketch was sailing about eighty degrees, a course that took it away from Montique. What they didn't know was that it took it closer to the submarine.

CHAPTER 9

The three of them slept around the clock without awakening once. The people from Grandau, grateful to have their princess back safely, looked after them, made sure they were comfortable, and waited for nature to wipe out their fatigue and bring back their youthful exuberance.

Most likely, it was the smell of breakfast that aroused them. The three of them were famished and ate heartily while Jon and Georg told how they were torn with the grief of their princess's disappearance, then bewildered when the boys were gone too. But from their mountaintop they had been able to witness what was going on. They saw the *Dragonfish* on the rocks and the boys' rescue of Tila, but they didn't dare interfere because something was happening there they didn't understand but the boys did. Then, when they saw the flames and the ketch retreating, they knew they could come down to complete the rescue.

Festivities were called for then. The old costumes were brought out, the cookfires kindled, and musical instruments from another age all transformed the top of Montique Island into the old and royal courtyard of Grandau. And Princess Tila of the House of Tynere and her two escorts were the chief guests of honor.

So great was the fun that hardly a person noticed the passing of the day until Helena, who was intrigued by Larry's binoculars and had been studying the terrain most of the time, came to the boys and pointed eastward across the ocean. She handed Larry the glasses and he adjusted the focus and looked out where she was pointing.

There, on the horizon, was the ketch. It was returning to Montique ... and following behind it was the long cylindrical shape of a submarine, its conning tower jutting skyward. He handed the glasses to Josh, and when he did the entire assembly went quiet.

"How much water does that submarine draw, Larry?"

"I doubt if they'll want to pass the fifty- or sixty-foot mark."

"Then they will have to stay at least two miles out there."

Larry's face looked glum. "We're well within range of their deck gun then. They can sit out there and pick us off like tin cans on the back fence."

Behind the mountain the sun had set and late dusk was about to give way to night. "Well," Josh said heavily, "at least we have tonight. There's not going to be much to shoot at until they get some light." He paused and shook his head sadly. "Boy, we don't have any luck at all. We think we've almost gotten them, then kerplooie! It all goes down the drain."

"Maybe not, Josh. Maybe not."

"How can you keep saying that, Larry?"

"There's still the *Tiger*."

"Come on ... we agreed not to tell these great people about sitting on top of a bomb like that."

"Not *tell* them," Larry said. "We're going to *show* them."

Josh was completely puzzled now. "Larry . . ."

"They all said it was a jinx ship, remember? But maybe it wasn't. Maybe it just was a ship that had a purpose. It saved the people from Grandau and later its longboat was there to get one of them out to tell the world the House of Tynere was ready to come home."

"But this is *now*, Larry!"

Larry wore a faint, faraway smile. He nodded in agreement with his friend's statement and said, "And *now* the *Tiger* is ready to finish her chosen assignment."

At first Josh thought his buddy had gotten a little too much excitement, but when Larry explained what he had in mind, the possibility of success dawned in his mind and he said, "It could work, Larry."

"It's all we have left."

"Let's get to it then!"

With the ever-present language barrier, the boys couldn't explain what they were going to do, but they were able to convey their excitement to the men, and while the women stayed on the mountaintop to protect their princess and light the smoke signal at the first light of dawn, the rest made torches to light their way down the path to the beach.

No longer did it matter if their lights were seen. They were trapped anyway, with no means of escape, and the enemy knew it so they could attack when they chose to. So the group went down the steep incline, the glare of the torches lighting their way. When they reached the beach they went toward the southern tip of it and Josh walked ahead. He called back, "The tide's going out, Larry. We'll have plenty of room."

Having already gone the route, the boys knew the way and the pitfalls to avoid, and this time they reached the cave entrance in a fraction of the time it had taken them earlier. There was one thing they had to do, however, and that was prepare the group for what they were about to see. The boys were so serious, their diagrams so complete, and the past events so vivid, that every man took them at their word and not one gave an unbelieving look.

But even so, when they stepped into that enormous chamber with the flaring torches shooting out yellow fingers of light, the sight they beheld froze them motionless, while their minds raced back over the stories that had come from their fathers and grandfathers.

Even after all these years, there was something majestic about that old square-rigged British ship of the line. She was an old lady, but she was still in her prime, her planking solid, her three masts tall and firm, with sails ready to billow out at the first touch of a breeze.

"This time we're going to have to go on board, Josh."

His friend said, "I know. We have to get the bowlines down to the men."

"If they're not rotted."

Josh's face creased in an optimistic grin. "I don't think the old girl would do that to us. Let's get up there."

The boys stood on the shoulders of Georg and Jon, were hoisted up to the open gunport, where they got a handhold on the cannon and a foot in the frame. From there they could reach the rail and they hauled themselves onto a deck that hadn't felt the feet of a human for two hundred years.

From where they stood the eerie sensation was greater than ever. It was as though the *Tiger* herself was watching every move they made and was making certain they made the right one. Something unspoken said that this was the hour of the *Tiger* . . . the very day it was built for. A long time ago she was commissioned to do something great. Not right then, but in the distant future, and for that event she had held herself in battle readiness until the true foe appeared; then she could go forward in her proud charge and do what she had to do.

Walking softly, not wanting to disturb the dignity of the moment, the boys tested the ropes coiled on the belaying pins, feeling the still-resilient tar woven into the fiber itself. "They're like new," Josh said.

"Toss them over, then. Make sure they're well secured on those forward bitts."

While Josh was at it Larry looked alive. There were two things he had to do. The first one took him to a small locker. Never before had he been near a ship like this, but it was as if he was being led. His fingers found the catch, opened the mahogany door, and reached in for the folded oblong canvas. He closed and latched the door, then went back to the mainmast. Unerringly, his fingers found the right line, unwound it from the cleat on the mainmast, and to the rings he attached the brightly colored canvas from the locker.

Every eye was watching him as he ran up the *Tiger*'s battle flag to the very tip of the mainmast and fastened the line on the cleat. From deep in the bowels of the ship there seemed to be a rumble of satisfaction. Josh had the lines over the side now and the men were holding them as they were instructed to.

Then Larry did the final thing he knew he had to do. He walked to that spot where the *Tiger*'s handsome engraved ship's bell was mounted and sounded it until the echoes reverberated from the walls of the great port that had hosted the guest ship all these years. Then he detached it, handed it over the side to Josh, clambered over the railing to the cannon mouth, and jumped to the ledge where the others were standing.

With the outgoing tide to help them, the men hoisted the lines on their shoulders and leaned into them. The initial motion was so slow they barely noticed it, then step by step the *Tiger* began to move toward the vaulted cave mouth, back to the sea she had left so long ago.

Once again the false dawn greeted them as the ship of the line moved past them from the momentum they had given it. There was no way she could be stopped now, and they shook the lines loose and watched her go by.

"Larry . . . we never set the sails. We didn't even know how to!"

"I don't think they have to be set, Josh. I think the *Tiger* knows exactly what she's doing. She managed a trip across the ocean all by herself and even found a safe harbor until she was needed. Now she's going out to do what she was designed for . . . fight and beat the enemy."

"That's a modern submarine out there, Larry, and the *Tiger*'s only an old wooden ship!"

As if to answer his statement, a morning breeze curled down from the mountain and filled the vast sail area, and the *Tiger* came alive with a glorious leap ahead that held for a minute; then, slowly, she

THE SHIP THAT NEVER WAS 111

turned and headed in a new direction slightly north-east of the island.

Josh could only stare, amazed. "Larry . . . she's sailing in the direction of the submarine!"

"I know," Larry said. He picked up the *Tiger*'s brass bell and waved everybody back on the path. As fast as they could, they made their way back to the beach. Just as they got there they heard the first high-pitched whine of a cannon shell go over the island, then a second that landed a hundred yards out in the ocean, throwing up a geyser of spray.

"They've got the island bracketed! The next one will come right in on it," Larry yelled. Nobody had to be told to dive for cover. The awesome noise of the shells and the explosion in the water told them what was happening. Now they had to wait for the final one.

The captain of the *Krolin* could hardly believe his eyes. The early low-hanging mist lifted just as he was about to give the command to fire the deck gun. From now on all the shells would be high explosive and he had figured that a dozen rounds would completely eliminate all signs of life from the island. But then this . . . this thing . . .

"What is it?" the mate asked anxiously.

"If I didn't know better I'd say it was an old British naval ship. Look, look." He pointed. "She's flying her colors and her battle flag!"

"Why would she do that?"

For a few minutes it didn't dawn on the captain. He stood there mute, watching a ship so antique she shouldn't be floating bearing down on them. And even that crazy island was doing something strange too. Now a thick tendril of smoke was going straight up into the fresh morning sky, a signal that would be visible for miles to ships and planes and could bring the wrath of nations down on his back if they were found here.

And the ship kept coming. Now he knew, all right. "She's going to attack us," he told his mate.

The mate had the *Tiger* in his field glasses. "An impossibility, Captain. She isn't even manned. Her decks are empty!"

"You fool, she's on a collision course and we can't maneuver!" He cupped his hand around his mouth and shouted to the gun crew. "There, *point-blank fire*! Stop that hulk . . . sink it!"

With empty eyes, Aktur Cilon and Embor Linero watched the fierce action as the crew swung the gun and aimed it. They could have told them it was no use, no use at all. The whole thing had been a jinx operation and now fate was laughing at them, and they knew that all the evil they had done had finally caught up with them.

The deck gun blasted that high-explosive shell at the hull of the *Tiger* rearing up above the highest point of the *Krolin*'s conning tower, and all Embor and Aktur could think of was, *How can you fight a ship that réally isn't there?*

The tremendous blast as the tons of unstable black powder in the hold of the *Tiger* exploded shook the island of Montique. From the shores they could see the mighty tongues of flame spit from the eruption of the fireball that boiled on the ocean's surface long seconds before gusting upward in a great draft of acrid black smoke.

When it was quiet again and the sky and water were clear, no one spoke a word. Out there the sea was serene, just as though nothing had ever happened at all. There was no ketch, no submarine, and no ship of the line with its battle flag snapping in the breeze.

Larry hefted the weight of the brass bell in his hand.

But there *had* been a *Tiger*.

From the top of the mountain they heard the warning horn, and in his glasses Larry saw Helena pointing out to sea. He turned his glasses in that direction and grinned.

"It's the *Blue Tuna*," he told Josh. "Just like our dads to get here after the action is over."

Two months later the helicopter landed at Peolle Island and a real princess stepped out with her guards, Georg and Jon, and her ladies-in-waiting, Margo and Helena. They had been two grueling months for the people of Grandau, coming back from the past to a renewed kingdom where they were eagerly awaited. Sir Harry had arranged for no mention of Embor and Aktur or the submarine to be made if Grandau was to be given complete freedom again. The dictatorship that held it considered it their best move and signed the papers of release.

Now they were going back, but before they left, it was the desire (and command) of Princess Tila that they see their old friends once again. It was supposed to be very special and very formal, but the three friends were filled with too much youth and vitality and they just grabbed at each other, jigging with happiness and trying to talk all at once.

And the boys were certainly surprised when they found that Tila had learned their language in those two months. Then the day was over and the party had to leave for Miami and the trip overseas.

Tila shook each boy's hand and said, "We're still friends, aren't we?"

"You bet," they agreed unanimously.

"Then I want you two to visit me in Grandau next summer. Will you do that?"

"Even if we have to swim," Josh said.

Behind them, Vincent whispered to his friend Tim, "They'd probably try it too. Maybe we'd better buy them tickets."

"I'm going to expect you, now. You two seem to know all about boats and the Caribbean and big cities on the mainland, but I want to show you where I live."

"But you don't even know what it's like," Larry said.

Tila smiled and drew herself erect. "Don't worry, I'll make it what I like," she told him.

"Just like a girl," Josh muttered playfully.

Then Larry brought up his package. He held it out and let Tila fold back the wrapping until the brass shone in the sunlight. "For you," he told her, "so you'll never forget us."

Slowly she pulled the cover all the way down and her eyes glistened with tears. It was the ship's bell from the *Tiger*, a secret that could never be told. Not that it mattered; it would never have been believed anyway. But the bell cemented a friendship among three people that could never be broken, and they all knew it well.

But it was a great story and for them it really had happened, even if it was a story about *the ship that never was*.

ABOUT THE AUTHOR

MICKEY SPILLANE is the nation's number one mystery story writer. His Mike Hammer mysteries have been instant successes since he first published in 1947.

The Day the Sea Rolled Back, his first novel for young people, was a Junior Literary Guild Selection. In *The Ship That Never Was* Mickey Spillane offers further proof of his marvelous ability to hold readers of any age spellbound.

Two thrilling and puzzling adventures from
America's #1 mystery writer
MICKEY SPILLANE

THE DAY THE SEA ROLLED BACK
(#14597-5 • $1.75)
Larry and Josh know where millions of dollars' worth
of treasure is hidden in the tropical waters surrounding
Peolle Island. But there doesn't seem any way to get
it. Then one day the sea goes out—and stays out.
Suddenly the race for the treasure is on. But Larry
and Josh aren't the only ones looking. Two treacherous
brothers will stop at nothing to get the riches for themselves.

THE SHIP THAT NEVER WAS
(#20380-0 • $1.95)
On a leisurely cruise around Peolle Island, Larry and
Josh discover a mysterious old longboat that appears to
be in perfect condition. And there's a man aboard
speaking in an ancient foreign language and carrying a
pouch of documents. Suddenly Larry and Josh are involved in finding a lost island . . . only somebody wants
to stop them *badly enough* to get rid of them forever.

DAHL, ZINDEL, BLUME AND BRANCATO

Select the best names, the best stories in the world of teenage and young readers books!

☐	20250	CHARLIE AND THE CHOCOLATE FACTORY Roald Dahl	$2.25
☐	20206	CHARLIE AND THE GREAT GLASS ELEVATOR Roald Dahl	$2.25
☐	12153	DANNY THE CHAMPION OF THE WORLD Roald Dahl	$1.95
☐	20172	THE UNDERTAKER'S GONE BANANAS Paul Zindel	$2.25
☐	12154	THE WONDERFUL STORY OF HENRY SUGAR AND SIX MORE Roald Dahl	$1.95
☐	14657	THE PIGMAN Paul Zindel	$2.25
☐	12774	I NEVER LOVED YOUR MIND Paul Zindel	$1.95
☐	14836	PARDON ME, YOU'RE STEPPING ON MY EYEBALL! Paul Zindel	$2.25
☐	12741	MY DARLING, MY HAMBURGER Paul Zindel	$1.95
☐	20170	CONFESSIONS OF A TEENAGE BABOON Paul Zindel	$2.25
☐	13628	IT'S NOT THE END OF THE WORLD Judy Blume	$1.95
☐	13693	WINNING Robin Brancato	$1.95
☐	12171	SOMETHING LEFT TO LOSE Robin Brancato	$1.75

Buy them at your local bookstore or use this handy coupon for ordering: